The All-American Boy

The
All-American Boy

A SCREENPLAY BY

Charles Eastman

FARRAR, STRAUS AND GIROUX
NEW YORK

The following still photographs are courtesy Charles
Eastman: cover; p. 66 top and bottom; p. 71 top and bottom;
p. 145 top and bottom; p. 147 bottom; p. 150 top and bottom.
All other still photographs are courtesy Warner Bros. Inc.

CAST (in order of appearance)

VIC BEALER: *Jon Voight*

CONNIE SWOOZE: *Nancie Phillips*

JAY DAVID SWOOZE: *Art Metrano*

SHEREEN BEALER: *Kathy Mahoney*

RODINE BEALER: *Carol Androsky*

NOLA BEALER: *Jeanne Cooper*

BETT VAN DAUMEE: *Peggy Cowles*

ARIEL VAN DAUMEE: *Bob Hastings*

JANELLE SHARKEY: *E. J. Peaker*

ARTY BALZ: *Ned Glass*

RING ANNOUNCER: *Ray Ballard*

DRENNA VALENTINE: *Anne Archer*

LARKEN: *Ron Burns*

PARKER: *Harry Northup*

POPPY: *Rosalind Cash*

ROCKOFF: *Gene Borkan*

LOVETTE: *Leigh French*

HIGH VALENTINE: *Jeff Thompson*

SARAGUSA: *Mac Chandler*

KNIPCHILD: *Owen Harlan*

MAGDA VALENTINE: *Jaye P. Morgan*

CREDITS

WRITTEN AND DIRECTED BY: *Charles Eastman*

PRODUCED BY: *Joseph T. Naar and Saul J. Krugman*

DIRECTOR OF PHOTOGRAPHY: *Philip Lathrop, A.S.C.*

UNIT MANAGER: *Nate Edwards*

ASSISTANT DIRECTOR: *Terry Morse, Jr.*

ART DIRECTOR: *Carey O'Dell*

SET DIRECTOR: *James I. Berkey*

SOUND: *Larry Jost*
MAKEUP SUPERVISOR: *Gordon Bau, S.M.A.*
HAIR STYLIST: *Jean Burt Reilly, S.H.S.*
MAKEUP TECHNICIAN: *Gary Liddiard*
POST PRODUCTION SOUND: *Arthur Piantadosi*
EDITORS: *Ralph Winters, Christopher Holmes, William Neel*
ASSISTANT EDITOR: *Joel Cox*
BOXING COACH: *Ric Mancini*
ASSISTED BY: *Charlie Powell, 'Cannonball' Green, Stoney Land*

Filmed in Panavision   Color by Technicolor
A My Shoes Production
Presented by Warner Bros., A Warner Communications Company

The All-American Boy

ONE

The Road to Buddy

This is a two-lane country road heavily grown on either side with weeds which half conceal the rusted wire and weathered wood of elderly fences. Black warty trees gesticulate from the slant of yellow hills that swell in the heat and tumble in every direction to the sun-dusted distance.

VIC BEALER comes along this way at midday, his plaid plastic suitcase banging against his knees as he looks for a ride that does not appear. All is silent except for his footsteps.

Why do we feel immediately that we recognize VIC? The slightly puffy brows over eyes that twinkle painfully. The movement of a body that favors the shoulders. A solid powerful body that pads forward when he walks in an oddly gentle, tentative way. A habitual merry feint of the head regardless of his mood. He is a boxer and though our realization of this is to come later, when closer views reveal scalp and brows scarred and calloused, now a flashy modesty of glance and stature tells us this much at least, that

3

vic is not just any person and that he is someone to whom being strong and handsome and always first seems an unfair advantage and embarrassing.

We follow vic as the road climbs slightly and twists to parallel a faintly green slope that gives evidence of being tended and is set now and then with a scattering of gravestones.

Buddy County Cemetery

This is actually the rear entrance of the cemetery that vic turns into, a steep gravelly road.

He hurries over the weedy graves where rusty coffee cans hold faded plastic daisies. An occasional squirrel dashes scarily across his path. It is very hot and he is sweating and his face is caked with dust and further darkened by a baffled grief.

Elsewhere in the Cemetery

This might be termed a better, more desirable area to be buried in, for it is moist and wooded and also thick with a company of more elaborate markers than those already seen, some profoundly phallic and some with Oriental markings.

vic walks fast and occasionally even breaks into a few running steps. This shortly feels unseemly to him in these surroundings, and so he settles back to a respectful if anxious trudge.

The Gravesite

The trees are new and spindly in this even more recent section of the cemetery, and most of the markers here are flat to the ground.

His suitcase banging heavily against his leg, VIC hurries toward the mourners he recognizes in the distance, bunched around the open grave and black as flies.

Swooze Living Room

Despite ample furnishings this room seems barren and unfinished still as though the owners were forever in the first year of their marriage. An ignorance of comfort dominates. Lamps and ashtrays are placed around with no thought to their function and dimestore paintings of remote waterfalls and concupiscent kittens are centered on each pastel green wall. A weakness for TV tables is evident, and yellow sports trophies adorn an otherwise empty bookcase.

VIC sits in a spindly rocker by the front door, open but screened, and with a look that resembles disgust, regards the sad group on the couch across the room from him:

His mother, NOLA BEALER, in dusty black; RODINE and SHEREEN, his sister-in-law and niece, in black maternity smock and frilly party dress, respectively—a wistful tableau, their hands interlocked.

Present as well is CONNIE SWOOZE, VIC's sister, also pregnant and also wearing black, and BETT VAN DAUMEE, who wears thick glasses and is dressed like a female cowboy.

BETT unloads a casserole and trimmings on the dining-room table as CONNIE, at the kitchen door, struggles into a plastic apron.

CONNIE

(Calling to the rear of the house) Jay David, you going to have time to eat something?

5

In the process of changing from his mourning clothes to work clothes, JAY DAVID SWOOZE appears briefly in the hall. He is very fat.

> JAY DAVID
>
> Just set up for them all. I'll eat something at the yard.

Behind JAY DAVID, ARIEL VAN DAUMEE enters. He is over forty but looks younger.

> ARIEL
>
> You going to pass up Bett's tamale pie?

He gestures to the others with an empty beer can.

> ARIEL
>
> Anyone else?

Getting no response, he exits to the kitchen and a fresh beer for himself.

> BETT
>
> How can you eat at the stockyards, Jay?

> CONNIE
>
> He could eat anywhere.

> BETT
>
> You ought to get up a petition against alienation of affection, Conn.

She goes to the kitchen for silverware.

> CONNIE
>
> Yeah, I'd like to know what that skinny bitch waitress has that Bett and I don't, Jay David.

She exits after BETT to the kitchen and JAY DAVID winks at the solemn clan in the living room.

I ain't telling.

He exits to the rear of the house.

NOLA gets stiffly to her feet.

> NOLA
>
> Anything I can do in there, Conn?

She too exits to the kitchen, leaving VIC, RODINE and SHER-
EEN alone in the living room.

> SHEREEN
>
> What if he comes alive in there?

> RODINE
>
> (Exhausted) What, honey?

> SHEREEN
>
> What if he does?

> RODINE
>
> Hush, Shereen.

> SHEREEN
>
> Is God mad at Daddy?

> RODINE
>
> No, honey. Now hush.

> SHEREEN
>
> Then how come he didn't let Daddy stay here?

VIC sits suddenly forward.

> VIC
>
> You keep that up, Shereen, and you're going to get a
> whipping, hear?

His words have come on him from nowhere, more vehement than he could explain. RODINE and SHEREEN look at him sharply. He gets to his feet as though to flee. But BETT comes in with a beer.

> BETT
>
> How's it going, Marlon? People still kid you about looking like Marlon Brando?

> VIC
>
> You're the only one ever says that, Bett.

She takes his arm, not seeing the fire that rages, and turns him to RODINE.

> BETT
>
> Don't he look like Marlon Brando, or am I nuts?

JAY DAVID comes in from the hall, dressed for work.

> JAY DAVID
>
> What about my nuts?

As CONNIE enters also.

> CONNIE
>
> *(Trying to avert an explosion)* Vic honey, would you put a leaf in the table for me?

> ARIEL
>
> You been getting any fights, Bomber?

> JAY DAVID
>
> What do you need a new leaf for? There ain't going to be but just you all.

> VIC
>
> Naw, I been taking it pretty easy.

> JAY DAVID
>
> *(Having stepped in it)* I mean, don't count on me is what I mean.

8

CONNIE

I just thought Brother might want to ask Janelle.

VIC mumbles negatively and extends the dining-room table.
ARIEL gives him a mock punch to the bicep.

ARIEL

Anything you want to do you know you got to keep
at, keep applying yourself.

JAY DAVID

(Pursuing his subject) She finds out you been in
town, Bomber, and she'll give you hell you didn't
call her up.

VIC

Hell, I'm only going to be here overnight.

NOLA comes in from the kitchen.

NOLA

Overnight?

VIC

I got to get back to L.A.

A look of concern passes from person to person. Until:

JAY DAVID

Why in hell you didn't call up so we could send you
plane fare—

VIC

Naw, heck.

NOLA

(Hopefully) You working?

VIC

I may sign up to work in Guam, I don't know yet.
They need construction workers over in Guam.

Again the anxious silence. Then:

ARIEL

> What Jay David means, Bomber, is you'd have more time to be home for a while if you'd just let us help you out.

VIC slams the table shut on the added leaf.

VIC

> What do I want to be home for? I don't want to be home.

Streets of Buddy

The sun beats down heavy and sad on these empty streets as VIC drives past shacks and churches and playgrounds and picket fences in a world without sidewalks.

We see no other human being and only an occasional car.

Countryside

A hone, unused for years, stands behind a barn, weeds grown up around it.

A dilapidated hut with the sign *Christmas Trees* painted on it in a white now weathered to chalk sags in the middle. In the foreground a rusted water tank lies on its side.

Through a rickety stable door, through two wide spaces between the planks, two anxious horses look out.

From high in the crotch of a tree, the view is of a tangled vineyard and an unclouded distance.

Poplar leaves flutter their gleaming currency in a startling breeze.

A deserted knoll worn with tire marks and scattered with empty flattened beer tins, rusted and sparkling in the sun. This is VIC's mountain, though it has been claimed likewise by other Buddians through the years. The tree trunks are carved with initials and dates going back to the forties.

VIC sits in the SWOOZE car here and stares into the valley. The view is of ochre hills punctuated with an occasional histrionic oak and clusters of cattle like driftwood or cloud. Shortly, he pulls the car around and drives off.

The walls of a concrete bridge over a small stream are painted with these spray-can legends: Sex Relieves Tension. Did You Conform. '57. D.M. '60. All Girls Look Better Naked. Boys Sure Don't.

Beside this bridge a road sign reads Buddy 7 El Deleria 30. The Swooze car, VIC at the wheel, appears, crosses the bridge and turns toward Buddy.

At another point along this stream the water gushes forward into ponds, deep and cold, and a pump whines from the lush bushes surrounding.

At another point still, canaled and geometric, this water transects a flat field of even alfalfa like a band of blue metal.

And finally there is nothing but the empty ruins of a municipal swimming pool with broken bottles on the bottom and tin cans and tennis shoes and a folding chair. A sign reading *No Trespassing* accents a silence broken only by the whimpering of a young dog that runs wildly back and forth along the edge of this pool, as though looking for a lost scent. Strange and out of place in this abandoned spot, the pup stops and bays at the sky for the someone who has left it. We hear also the sound of a man weeping.

11

Main Street

Though not literally Main Street, this is Central Buddy, fixed and dingy as the fringes of town proliferate with liquor store and laundrymat and gas station and supermarket.

VIC parks and gets out of the car.

The temperature in Buddy from early spring until almost winter is in the nineties most days. It is today. So VIC has the sidewalks to himself as he moves past shop windows decorated with dead flies, shops that are printing businesses and distributors of items not much in demand, or are merely empty in buildings of crumbling brick.

Buddy Drugstore

This is indeed to step into the past where pasteboard doctors and glossy people in pain crowd the aisles and counters, and smiling ladies, curly and flushed and one-dimensional, perform a public toilet.

VIC crosses to a black-and-purple tile fountain and sits down at a sign reading *Closed*. He stares at his knuckles, his tired eyes as mean as he is hurt. At the end of the counter, pouring over movie magazines, two young girls enrich the heavy quiet with their buzz and twitter.

Elsewhere in the drugstore, an elderly pharmacist talks on the phone behind the muffling effect of a glass prescription booth, and at the cash register JANELLE SHARKEY, in lofty coif and cosmetician's uniform, concludes impatiently with a cowed customer.

In more sophisticated surroundings JANELLE SHARKEY would go unnoticed. But in Buddy her superior airs establish her as someone born for a better fate than to languish on the vine in San Joaquin. And if by nothing else this

12

stardom is confirmed by her relationship with VIC, tenuous as it mostly is.

She leans now coolly against the fountain beside him, a position she takes to keep an eye on the pharmacist, who, looking up, would see them, no doubt disapproving of personal visits on company time.

> VIC
>
> You don't seem any real surprised.

> JANELLE
>
> I only got three calls in the last half hour.

> VIC
>
> Oh, crap this town.

The pharmacist disappears momentarily beneath the counter and JANELLE leans quickly down and kisses VIC. Then just as quickly she straightens up and the pharmacist reappears. She turns and stares at herself in the fountain mirror.

> JANELLE
>
> Everyone wanting to know if I knew you was back and how come you hadn't called me up yet and if we broke up or what.

> VIC
>
> What business is it of everybody's?

> JANELLE
>
> That's what I told them.

> VIC
>
> Just don't tell me who or I'll break their backs.

> JANELLE
>
> Bett van Daumee for one. And Rockoff seen you driving out to the stockyards with Jay David.

VIC

I had to drive him to work, that's all.

JANELLE

It just makes me sick.

VIC

So what's going on, anything?

JANELLE

I knew you'd call when you were ready, that's all.

VIC

Well, I'm ready.

JANELLE

First off, Vic, I just don't know what to say.

VIC

That's all right.

JANELLE

So I'm just not going to try and say anything, all right?

VIC

All right.

JANELLE

About Larry, I mean.

VIC

Been hot? What's the weather been like?

JANELLE

It was just such a shock, that's all.

VIC

What's been going on? Anything? Been up to the lake?

JANELLE

The main thing I got to know is how are you?

VIC

You know the last time I was asleep?

JANELLE

You want to come over to my house?

VIC

Now?

JANELLE

And sleep.

VIC

Yeah, what about your dad?

JANELLE

He won't get off till after seven. He's working days again.

VIC

Days, huh? That's pretty great. How's he like working days for a change?

JANELLE

Only I'll have to come back and work tonight if I get off now. That's the only thing. Did you have plans for tonight?

The tide of pain rises again in VIC and he looks from side to side as though to find a place to spill it.

JANELLE

You okay?

VIC

Maybe I just better not be with nobody today, Janelle, okay?

JANELLE

I'll just tell him I'll be back after supper and then I'll be back, okay?

JANELLE departs, and VIC stares in blind hurt down the counter toward DRENNA VALENTINE, one of two girls at the magazine rack—a spirited tomboy in jeans and sweatshirt who returns his look over the top of *Stag* or *Bachelor* or *Gory Gentleman.*

JANELLE comes back removing her smock.

JANELLE

(Sharply to DRENNA *and her accomplice)* If you're not going to buy those, you kids, you're not supposed to be reading them.

The girls gloomily return the magazines to the rack and prepare to depart.

VIC

(Desperately) I just feel I'd like to do something bad. Just bite down on something hard and break it.

But he allows himself to be led as JANELLE takes his arm and all but lifts him from his seat.

Main Street

VIC and JANELLE come from the drugstore and cross toward the Swooze car, where PARKER, LARKEN and ROCKOFF wait.

Sweating and slow with sleeplessness, VIC nods gratefully at the embarrassed shuffling of his buddies. Several moments pass. Finally:

PARKER

How are you, Janelle?

JANELLE

(*To* VIC) Come on, honey.

ROCKOFF

Twenty-nine years old. Shit. And I just seen him last week.

VIC

See you guys later, okay?

ROCKOFF

I said hi and he said hi. And now it's all over.

VIC

Yeah wull, what else is there to do in this damn town but screw, booze and smash up, Rockoff? Nothing.

He pulls JANELLE to his side in an almost contemptuous embrace. Then he opens the car door for her and she gets in. He follows.

Swooze Car Interior

Where the sun has hit the seat, it is scorching. Also the glass and paneling. VIC takes the wheel, carefully at first.

JANELLE

Hot?

Then he grips it hard, welcoming the pain. He makes no move to start the car.

JANELLE looks out uneasily at PARKER, LARKEN and ROCK-OFF watching from the sidewalk. And down the street, DRENNA and her friend stare as well in solemn interest from a jeep.

Vic?

He doesn't answer. He stares at his hands. He is trembling.

JANELLE

Honey?

Janelle's Bedroom

It is hot and the windows are open and a sprinkler watering the back lawn plays against the screen. The windowsill is damp and a faint breeze wafts the frilly curtains.

VIC and JANELLE, dewed with sweat and the cooling moisture from outside, are on the floor between the bed and the window.

VIC

(Suddenly) What?

JANELLE

Were you asleep?

VIC

N'uh'uh.

JANELLE

Can I just say something?

VIC

If a house is on fire and you can't get out you're supposed to lie on the floor if you can't get any air.

JANELLE

I just want you to know, honey, that you're free.

VIC

Okay.

18

JANELLE

And I am too. *(Silence)* It's just I don't want you to
feel like you're tied down or anything.

VIC

Okay.

JANELLE

Especially now. *(Silence)* Because I know how you
feel.

VIC

Thanks, Janelle.

JANELLE

Were you asleep?

VIC

What?

JANELLE

I thought you were awake.

VIC

No, I appreciate that.

JANELLE

Don't go to sleep.

VIC

Don't. I smell.

JANELLE

You smell like cantaloupe.

VIC

Hell, Janelle, you're strange.

JANELLE

What are you, too sleepy?

                              VIC

I'm never too sleepy.

                              JANELLE

You keep on falling asleep.

                              VIC

Just go on without me if I fall asleep, okay?

                              JANELLE

Sometimes I feel so cheap, you know, Vic. I just
think about you all the time you're away and wish
you were here so hard. Vic?

                              VIC

What?

                              JANELLE

What are your plans?

VIC stands up.

                              VIC

I'm going to take a shower.

He stumbles stiffly toward the bathroom. JANELLE follows
him.

                              JANELLE

No, I mean, what do you think you'll do about the
future?

Bathroom

VIC turns on the shower as JANELLE appears behind him.

                              JANELLE

Do you think you'll go to work for Ariel or with Jay
David or what?

She stuffs her hair into a shower cap.

20

VIC

Boy, everybody sure is interested in what I'm going
to do with my future.

He climbs into the shower.

Shower

VIC faces the consoling water. JANELLE joins him.

JANELLE

Ariel says if you really wanted to, you could really
get to be somebody.

VIC

Get to be?

JANELLE

That's what he tells everybody.

She circles his waist with her arms and rests her head
against his chest as the water pours over them.

JANELLE

That he wouldn't take no one for you.

She hugs him tightly.

JANELLE

And me either. Me too.

He reaches for the soap, attempting to disengage himself.

VIC

How come everybody's all of a sudden so interested
in what I'm going to do with myself?

JANELLE

You won't tell anyone this, will you?

VIC

Naw, heck. What?

21

That we took a shower together. I feel like such a whore.

The Pastime

This is a long narrow bar and restaurant related in feeling to the Western saloon. At one end is a piano bar, though no pianist. VIC and ARIEL sit here, having had several beers.

ARIEL

When do you absolutely have to be back?

VIC

Hell, I guess I'll take off in the morning.

ARIEL

I don't see why so soon. You want another beer? Hey, Joe, another beer over here.

VIC

(After a moment) I ain't coming back to Buddy, Ariel.

ARIEL

Oh, I didn't know that. Is that right? I didn't know that. Is that what you're announcing? *(Silence)* Well, I know Larry was thinking that you was planning . . . I don't know. I just know he took a lot of pride in the Club, that's all . . . and . . . *(Then)* Well, I just want you to know, Vic, what Larry had with me you got now. You know that, don't you?

VIC

Which is what, Arie? Nothing.

ARIEL

No, heck. Journeyman's good wages, clean work.

VIC

You ain't working, Ariel. You spend more time in that crappy Boys' Club that nobody appreciates—

ARIEL

Well, like me and Larry always figured, it was worth it if you had a place to train if you ever decided you wanted to take advantage, Vic, of who you are.

VIC

I'm nobody, hell.

ARIEL

How's Janelle?

VIC

I'm not even a good guy.

ARIEL

One thing you can say about marriage is it puts your feet on the ground and you get more conscious of your goals, seems like.

VIC

Yeah wull, that's what they're trying to do too, isn't it?

ARIEL

Who?

VIC

Life. Is put everybody in a cage and then they'll be satisfied.

ARIEL

I just feel you'd be more sure of your goals, that's all. In life.

VIC

You'd be more sure about me, you mean.

NOLA appears from the kitchen carrying VIC's dinner. The starched and jaunty, too youthful uniform she wears is a costume almost comical but for the plaintive no-nonsense of her manner.

ARIEL

We just all hate to see you drift your time away, Vic, like this is what we just all hate to see you do. When you got such a potential, just to throw it all away on Guam.

NOLA puts VIC's food before him. She sits down opposite him, across the piano. He eyes her fiercely.

VIC

God is poppycock.

NOLA

Is that right?

VIC

No, I mean it.

NOLA

There'll be lots of people relieved to have the final word on that.

VIC

Okay. Okay.

She pushes salt and pepper and steak sauce at him.

NOLA

After all these years of stumbling around in the dark.

VIC

Okay, never mind.

24

NOLA

You want some milk?

ARIEL

Hey, Joe, where's the Bomber's beer?

VIC

Because everyone's trying to get everyone to believe that it's God's will that Larry got killed.

NOLA

I don't think anybody here needs any more beer.

VIC

When all it was was damn dumb Larry out to El Deleria cutting up.

ARIEL

Have some consideration for your mother, Vic.

VIC

You know Larry, Mom, he was just drunk, wasn't he?

NOLA

Eat your dinner, son.

VIC

(Instant appreciation) Gee, heck, yeah. Didn't think I was this hungry, wow, for a steak. What's this, the best steak in the house?

ARIEL

I'll take it then if you don't want it.

VIC

Hell you will. Just try it.

JOE SARAGUSA, the Pastime's bartender and proprietor, arrives with a fresh beer for VIC.

NOLA

I better see if Trish and Augie want anything.

There has been intermittent giddy laughter from a rear booth.

SARAGUSA

They're fine. Just take it easy, stay where you are.

NOLA

No, I'm fine.

SARAGUSA

You got a great old lady here, Vic.

VIC

You don't have to tell me that.

SARAGUSA departs.

VIC

Except I'd sure like to know what she's trying to prove.

NOLA

No need for Joe to be shorthanded on account of me. Situation normal is always the best in my book.

She moves down the bar to the booth from whence the laughter comes.

VIC eats and then looks up at ARIEL, who has been strangely silent.

ARIEL

I'm not drunk.

VIC

I didn't say you was drunk.

ARIEL

But if I was I would be very proud to be.

VIC

Boy, this town.

ARIEL

This town, this town—what the hell kind of remark is that to keep on making?

VIC regards him and his strange, out-of-nowhere, puny anger.

ARIEL

What's this town got to do with anything? Same town it always was.

VIC

Hell it is.

ARIEL

Don't pull that on me, Vic Bealer.

VIC

I didn't say you was drunk. I said I was drunk.

ARIEL

He was my partner and if he was standing right here right now and I was dead I'd want him to be dead drunk too if he was any friend of mine's. Because don't think I didn't love that guy. Like I love every one of you blessed Bealers.

VIC

He could of really been something, Ariel.

ARIEL

Goddamnit, Larry was something, Vic.

VIC

A sucker.

ARIEL

No sir, he was a fine man.

VIC

He was a nice guy with a nice wife but a brat kid and a house somebody else has got to pay off now and a car now he's through with it no one else can use.

ARIEL

He had a good life. Larry had a good life.

VIC

I don't call buried in the American Legion section of the Buddy County Cemetery any good life, I'm sorry.

ARIEL gets up and starts for the jukebox.

ARIEL

What's your favorite song? You got a quarter?

VIC

Because that's what you're saying, isn't it? Put yourself in a tie and union dues and all that crud and insurance policies and all that crud and which that ain't life, Ariel. And straightening the baby's teeth, that ain't life.

ARIEL

What's life, Vic? I don't know.

VIC

Well, it's not never getting all the plaster out of your hair and even on Sundays smelling of paint.

VIC looks at his brother's friend with a sadness that is almost nausea and ARIEL involuntarily reaches to his hair, spotted slightly with plaster and smelling of paint.

TWO

Downtown Los Angeles

His plaid plastic suitcase a burden ignored, VIC moves intently along these streets among the disgruntled sidewalk spitters and the blue-suited businessmen as spirited as nuns at recess; he wears spruce wash 'n' wear slacks and sports shirt and lopes through parking lots and past used clothing stores with a by now familiar earnestness that is almost urgency. Elderly Mexican women, heavily laden but inconspicuous, impede his stride.

He stops and spots his destination across the street; then in a dancing half-run he crosses through the traffic, his suitcase banging against his calf.

He approaches a building identified as *The New Avenue Walkup Gym and Cultural Center, Arty Balz, Manager.*

He stands before this building briefly intimidated, and then enters and goes up the stairs.

Gym

It is early and everything is still and echoey and a growling voice floats down from above: ARTY BALZ on the phone in his office.

> ARTY
>
> *(Off stage)* So I just look at him, see, and listen, but I wouldn't go four thousand for a guy like that . . .

VIC pauses and not knowing what else to do reads from a bulletin board while the voice continues from overhead.

> ARTY
>
> *(Off stage)* Pig in a poke. Because he's young and he don't know what he's going to do.

VIC idles forward.

> ARTY
>
> *(Off stage)* So I said, you don't have a green one-hundred-and-forty-pounder, do you—white or black, but green. Or not green. A good fighter even. I could use a good fighter by Sunday. Or green. *(Concluding)* And tell him does he want to go to San Diego.

He hangs up and comes fuming into the gym.

> ARTY
>
> Fucking bastards.

He sees VIC.

30

ARTY

What the hell do you want?

VIC

Cost anything to watch the workouts for a while?

ARTY

What the hell. Fifty cents. This ain't no free show, for Christ's sake.

VIC puts his suitcase down and digs deep for money.

ARTY

I don't know who's here yet. Don't no one usually show up this early.

He takes VIC's money and returns to his office, mumbling muffled oaths.

ARTY

And don't touch none of the equipment neither.

Alone, VIC sits down and surveys the area around him, the walls lined with full-length mirrors and stained, moldy portraits of former boxing greats. There is a large ring at the other end of the room and many punching bags and tables and along the walls more seats, presumably for spectators.

VIC clears his throat and waits, staring agreeably into the empty, echoing, redolent space.

A Mexican bantamweight enters, carrying a small valise which holds his gear. He has the air we have already observed in VIC of going softly, of modest apology for the prowess and strength that set him apart, a need to be inconspicuous. He looks around as though he'd never been here before and then disappears into the dressing rooms.

31

An electric bell sounds and continues hereafter at intervals corresponding to actual rounds.

VIC, elsewhere than when we left him, clears his throat again and takes a speck of dust off his polished shoes.

Now an older Latin is nearby. He leans against the wall, his feet up on the seat next to him, and drinks from a paper cup of steaming coffee.

Now the bantamweight, wearing blue wool trunks, is in the ring, shadowboxing.

Another fighter watches. Young, handsome to the point of prettiness, and still in street clothes he lies face down on one of the tables waiting to get into the mood to work out.

There is the sound of the bantamweight's feet dancing on the mat and his soft snorting breath.

ARTY crosses the gym to answer the phone ringing in his office as two black fighters enter, one carrying a child on his shoulders.

> ARTY
>
> (Off stage) Shit, sure he's signed. The originals are with the Commission and the yellows they got and I seen the blues down at the office myself.

Put on his feet, the black child surveys the gym importantly. The Latin trainer near VIC scrounges up in comic imitation of fear that the child will hit him. Neither the child nor his handsome parent reacts to this playfulness.

The pretty fighter emerges from the locker room, having lost his glamour in removing his clothes; a tacky satin robe, almost in shreds, shrouds him now.

ARTY addresses the Latin while hungrily scanning the gym for signs of injustice or treachery.

ARTY

Shit, those guys can't hurt each other, he tells me, and I say shit who's he kidding. Because Gordy if he wants to can kill that motherfucker. And you're just praying, Mr. Calamore, I told him, you're just praying he won't let go.

An enormous Negro ties the pretty fighter's hand wraps and then approaches ARTY and the almost sleeping Latin.

BIG FISH

Stand back and let the big fish swim.

Though they might see each other here every day and any night there's a fight in town, still they shake hands all around as though it has been weeks; and ARTY turns to appraise the pretty fighter, girlish and virginal, jumping rope before the mirror, his damp dirty shorts flapping like a limp skirt; and ARTY's look is more envious for seeming to sneer.

The bell continues to sound at intervals, more frequent now, and is louder as well. The sound of punching bags adds to this music and, swinging slowly against the full light of the windows, the mounting ballet of shape and shadow. And the soft thud of the pretty fighter's feet and the rope slapping the mat. And the snorting of the bantam-weight shadowboxing.

An elderly trainer pulls hand wraps off a young fighter, the gauze like streamers in the air.

BIG FISH wraps his boy in the embrace of a heavy towel and rubs him. A cigar extended from his otherwise tuskless

33

mouth, he conspires with a silk-suited matchmaker who chews on a pair of horn-rimmed glasses and squints at the flesh around him with a jeweler's eye.

In the far corner of the room an eerie youth stares into the air, lifeless and waxen. He is punchy or an addict—which? In any case, he is lost. His clothes are secondhand and too big for him. Strangely his shoes are bright and shiny and very sharp. He mumbles to himself.

The faces of these fighters . . . they are young. Apple faces, fierce yet somehow feminine. They have a kind of innocence about them, a soft lifelessness that suggests they can live only in the hothouse of the gym.

Yet, looking further, this modest quality is not found in all. Some here are cocky, and assume a celebrity or their right to it simply in donning trunks and gloves and taking in the hopes of tired trainers.

And some are not so young after all as we see them closer, but are seedy and sad and need haircuts and are sleazy and past their prime though they may be only twenty-five. It is these who bring along their women friends to watch them work out and who would be nothing without a mirror.

The elderly trainer is now rolling up the used hand wraps, one end tied to the ring while the other is carefully rolled. The first to admit his lack of station, this man makes much of staying out of people's way and mumbles uncalled-for apology at every turn and so is hard to overlook.

There is a young Mexican, fat and fourteen, here for correctional gym. And an Indian (or Negro in disguise) wearing a cheap white turban. And a Marine, redheaded where he is not bald, making contacts for service bouts.

The sound of the bell is now accelerated.

The punching bags are all in motion, corpse-like and gloomy against the windows.

The pictures on the wall of yellowed old-timers are equally lifeless and spooky.

The shower room echoes wetly shrieks and curses.

A fighter grunts fiercely at himself in the mirror.

A jump rope slaps the floor repeatedly.

Wet gray silk shorts cling to the skin of wagging hips like old bandages.

A fighter spits into a funnel.

A worn woman turns away, fingering her neck nervously to see a Filipino poke at his crotch with a gloved hand.

The eerie youth stares ahead from his seat in the corner, smiling faintly. A drunken Negro next to him chuckles and wags his head, feeling he has found a friend when it is catalepsy which suffers his encroachment, nothing more.

VIC clears his throat nervously, about to take some as yet undetermined action.

The matchmaker gnaws his glasses thoughtfully and puts a benign hand on the head of the Negro child, an advance on the black parent they each regard, stunning at his workout.

BIG FISH, rubbing down the pretty fighter, grabs ARTY, who hurries across the gym in response to the renewed ringing of the phone.

> BIG FISH
>
> Who's that mother?

ARTY looks and we see that it is VIC, out of place if not illegal in street clothes, punching the farthest bag.

35

ARTY

These guy, these fucking bastards. I told him not to
touch nothing or he'd have me to tangle with.

BIG FISH

Hold on. If he's off the street I want to talk to that
mother.

The result of this interest is that ARTY reevaluates VIC.

ARTY

What do you mean, the street? Hell, that's my new
boy, you bastard.

BIG FISH

Hell your new boy. You never seen that mother before, Arty.

ARTY

What are you talking about? Damn, that's my new
fighter. Didn't I tell you I found me a new boy?

Vermont Street, Night

A bus pulls up to the curb and VIC and ARTY, among others,
get out, VIC with his suitcase. It is night. VIC wears a wind-
breaker.

They walk up Vermont toward City College, ARTY coughing, spitting and shaking his head darkly against the
world's injustices.

ARTY

Not a cocksucker ever gave me a dime. But they said
they did.

VIC looks around uncomfortably each time a profane note is
struck, expecting to find an outraged eavesdropper.

I'm a matchmaker, I told him, how am I to know if the bastard's a guild member. So they took away the TV Main from me. I made the TV Main and they took it away from me. And now then they were butting in on my preliminaries and poking around.

City College

They turn onto the deserted campus, and as they are the only strollers along these sparsely lighted lanes, their footfalls and their voices clearly echo.

ARTY

Oh, you got to watch out for them bastards, Curley, I'm warning you.

VIC

Only I don't pay no attention.

ARTY

Because they're going to be coming after you, seeing what you got.

VIC

Yeah, but they're not going to get me, though.

ARTY

Oh hell no, I know I don't have to worry about you. I just wanted to warn you. People are going to want a piece of you and you got to be prepared for that.

VIC

You keep calling me Curley.

ARTY

Cocksuckers.

vic turns aside to conceal a grin.

ARTY

What the hell are you smiling about?

VIC

Nothing. Sometimes I smile. I don't even know why.

They pass through the ivied arches of North Hall and head for the blunt moonlit concrete gym.

ARTY

In 1927 I gave Slapsy Maxie twenty dollars to fight for me out of Chicago, and look what he went on to.

VIC

I know I probably heard of you, if I could only just remember.

ARTY

And old George Raft bought one of my boys.

VIC

Is that right?

ARTY

You're goddamn right.

VIC

Old George who?

Football Field

Immobilized by moonlight, they stand in the center of this vast grassy oval.

ARTY

This here is where you'll roadwork. Leastwise until

38

school starts and then you'll have to get up before six if you want to use it or they'll kick you off.

VIC

What do you have to be, going to school to get on the team?

ARTY

To hell with school, forget it.

VIC

No, you ought to see my shelf, no kidding.

ARTY

Your shelf?

VIC

Wull, me and my brother used to have what we called our trophy shelf—

ARTY

Shit trophies.

He departs and VIC follows.

VIC

Wull, it was just kid stuff but—

ARTY

Boxing is the only education anyone needs.

Arty's Street

VIC and ARTY cross toward a dark bungalow near the corner.

ARTY

Boxing is the greatest education to come down to man.

39

VIC

There's lots of people think it's violent, though.

ARTY

The greatest education, the greatest science, the greatest religion, the greatest art.

VIC

You know what my mother says?

ARTY

All that crap, if people only knew it.

VIC

That she could understand it better if it was two against one.

ARTY

You send your mother to me.

VIC

No, she was only kidding.

Arty's House

They go up onto the porch.

ARTY

Fighting is a art, you tell her that.

VIC

Naw, she was just kidding. She likes to kid me all the time.

ARTY

One bastard working all alone to take care of hisself and using everything he is. You tell her that.

He pokes at the lock with a stubborn key.

40

VIC

She'd wash my mouth out, I talk like you do, Arty.

ARTY

Key-reyst!

VIC

What's the matter?

ARTY

Goddamn motherfucking son-of-a-bitch key won't
fit. *(Then, amazed)* Oh.

The door opens, all the time unlocked.

ARTY

Come on in.

Living Room

VIC is silhouetted in the doorway as ARTY stumbles through
the dark, knocking into things and cursing.

VIC

I sure do incidentally appreciate . . . I mean what
I'll probably do, Mr. Balz, is get a job right away
and then be able to pay you—

ARTY

Never mind about any fucking jobs—

He switches the light on.

ARTY

Just close the door.

He approaches and slams the door behind VIC.

ARTY

Before all the fucking moths get in.

He crosses to the rear of the house.

ARTY

And don't call me Mr. Balz.

VIC follows.

Bedroom

Ducking self-consciously, VIC enters, after ARTY, a small room with a desk, a sagging bed, and an easy chair with no pillow in the seat.

ARTY

You want a radio?

VIC

Naw, heck. This'll be great.

ARTY

No, I'll put a radio in so you can listen to the radio.

Shuddering in an excitement he would likely deny, ARTY exits for the radio.

ARTY

Kids like to listen to the radio.

VIC studies the dismal room. On the windows bamboo curtains are arched and buckled and coming apart.

VIC

(Up) You're not married or anything? I mean your wife's not going to mind I just barging in?

ARTY returns with the radio.

ARTY

Shit, what do I want to get married for?

VIC

It's just I don't want to be no trouble.

ARTY

It's no trouble, it's portable.

He crouches down and searches under the bed for a plug.

VIC

Because I don't have no way of paying you back just
now until I do.

ARTY

Hell, Curley, I'd sooner that you owed me than you
didn't have time to train or was too fucking tired
out. That's the whole point.

VIC

You keep calling me Curley.

ARTY

A kid like you just deserves somebody takes a interest in you, that's all.

He finds the plug and returns to view.

ARTY

What's your favorite program? I don't know even
what's on.

VIC shakes his head in incredulous gratitude that somehow
doesn't quite ring true.

VIC

Boy, how come people are so good to me everywhere
I'm at.

ARTY, still on his knees, looks up at him.

ARTY

I see the kind of kid you are, good clean kid you are.

43

VIC can't meet this gaze.

> VIC
>
> Yeh, wull heck . . . no, sure, Arty, I'll pay you back.

> ARTY
>
> You'll pay me back. I ain't worried.

> VIC
>
> Well then, good night I guess, okay?

ARTY gets to his feet.

> ARTY
>
> And don't forget to say your fucking prayers.

He goes and VIC sits down and stares at the floor.

Football Field

VIC runs backwards, light on his feet and indefatigable, his breath hoarse and visible in the early morning air.

When the sun is finally risen, he surrenders, soaked and steaming, to ARTY's routinely critical embrace and is roughed up in a robe and heavy towels.

Arty's Back Yard

Naked but for shorts, and dappled in sunlight, VIC lies on a redwood picnic table under an arbor of ivy. His head bobs loosely, as ARTY rubs him down.

> VIC
>
> How come you ain't married, Arty? Your wife die or something?

44

ARTY

Shit, I told you, what do I want to get married for

VIC

Man, you're something else.

ARTY

I never seen all the need for all that sexual.

VIC

You can't even say two words without one of them being a cuss word.

ARTY

People make too much out of it.

VIC

That's all the vocabulary you got is cuss words.

ARTY

All I need with you. That's all you'll listen to.

VIC

Tell me something I don't know some day and then I will.

ARTY

Okay. Turn your butt over.

VIC

See what I mean? And you're supposed to be an example.

He turns over on his stomach.

ARTY

Butt ain't no cuss word.

VIC stares at the ground for some time. The sun and ARTY's fingers tranquillize and ease the defenses of a sore subject.

VIC

I walked out on my marriage. Right the day out of it. I just called up and shipped out.

ARTY

Good for you.

VIC

I don't know, though.

ARTY

That's one thing you don't need is all that crap.

VIC

It's a bad deal, though, not to when you said you would. *(Then)* But I just knew I wouldn't. So I just walked out. *(Then)* Maralue . . . Merilee . . . I don't even remember her name. Something like that. And her bathing suit was polka-dot.

ARTY

Hell, she's better off not married if it's to you.

VIC leans down to adjust his radio, handy on the redwood bench.

VIC

Marilyn . . . Merilee . . . Something like that. And I told her I had to go around the world. Walked right out of it, right the day out of it, when I told her all along I would.

ARTY

It's not the first girl it's happened to.

VIC

No, she was a decent girl. Mary Lee or Mary something. I've never even told this to no one.

ARTY

It happens.

46

Larry'd came all the way down here. Dropped his job and came all the way here when I called him up and told him. And we just shipped out and went on home. And she didn't even say don't when I called her up and told her I had to go around the world instead of marrying her.

ARTY

What was she, pregnant?

VIC

Meridee, that's what it was. Meridee, and I was out of school and bumming around and I had already been in seventeen states. I don't even know why I'm telling you this but I did. Knocked her up and then called her up and said goodbye because Larry'd came to get me.

ARTY

He really loved you. I wish I had a brother.

VIC

He gave me a bum steer.

ARTY

No, he didn't want you to mess up your life.

VIC

I wrote her a letter.

ARTY

Merida?

VIC

Not just one letter either. I wrote her every day all summer and I'm not any letter writer either. But I did. They'd closed the plunge because of polio and I put in all these things that I was feeling, what I would do for her if I could because I knew she got a raw deal and I wanted her to know I knew she did.

ARTY

She write back?

VIC

Hell, I never even sent them. Hell, I never even had
her address. I didn't even know her last name or her
front name for sure. And now between us both we
probably got some little kid walking around could
be eight years old.

ARTY

It's a woman's function to get married.

VIC

(Darkly) And everybody says the great Vic Bealer.

ARTY

I feel sorry for them.

VIC

They always want to get married.

ARTY

Well, it's their function in life.

VIC

And they're just waiting around for it to happen
and it's urgent but they can't even show it. It's
rough. I feel sorry for them. I mean, that's their
whole life, a man.

ARTY

Okay—up.

VIC sits up and ARTY takes his arm and pulls it soothingly
from its happy socket. VIC yawns.

Whereas at least a man has got his work.

El Monte Legion Stadium

A standard elevated ring in the middle of a large room, with several rows of folding chairs around it. At one end of the room is a stage with some partitions set up. It is here that the fighters must change, in view of any in the audience who care to look. What little theater or the high-school play is to the student actor, this event is to the novice boxer.

VIC, scented and starched and carrying his gear in a small valise, is halted halfway across the stage by a scratchy recording of *The Star-Spangled Banner*. ARTY is behind him, and other fighters and their managers, giving token respect to God and country.

As it happens, VIC is standing directly under the flag and it would appear as though the audience were focused on him, singing to him. He clears his throat, therefore, and steps back uncomfortably, seeking the shadows. However, this vantage, if accidental, is not undesirable as far as ARTY is concerned. Pretending to rub VIC's shoulder, he shoves his fighter forward once again as the anthem crests toward conclusion.

ARTY

(Harsh whisper) Hey, you guys, button up, will you? Love it or leave it, for Christ's sake.

This to BIG FISH in the background, who, sotto voce, talks to the Latin trainer. And taking small steps, ARTY moves in that direction, only now and then holding still for form's sake and saluting.

The record concludes and vɪc catches up with ARTY in the dressing area and there, as though preparing for an operation, he lays out his gear along a bench: his trunks, his mouthpiece, and not least of all his radio.

ARTY

I don't know who you drew or actually who showed up but it probably won't be much of a war unless you get one of those Navy guys.

vɪc turns his radio on loudly, as though to discourage further talk. He doesn't appear to be nervous: simply remote, unreachable. If pushed, however, the violence of his impending encounter in the ring is ready to advance in the form of temperament. Furthermore, he is ever formidable, even when most easy going and one habitually gives him room. Thus ARTY turns to BIG FISH and the Latin again.

ARTY

Hey, you bastards, I thought you was going to give us a lift out here.

Meanwhile in the ring an ANNOUNCER reaches for a descending microphone.

ANNOUNCER

Good evening, ladies and gentlemen and fight fans young and old. The Olympic Development Club of Southern California welcomes you all to this second in the series of Olympic Development matches in Southern California . . . the winner to contest up north at a later date. We are proud tonight to have six boys from the San Diego Naval Base up here to meet with a few local boys and a few boys who this will be their first fights that we are keeping all our eyes on who are interested in seeing the United

States stay ahead in the upcoming Olympics and seeing the free world come up with some good punching boys able to defend ourselves against anybody.

Under this we visit the blushing warriors already prepared for the early bouts, tender boxers who sit along the stage or stand waiting: hand-wrapped boys in trunks, some in swimsuits, some in bathrobes; some sharpies even have their own silks. A few have regulation headgear. All have seconds, older managers or hero-worshipping kids their own age. Some shadowbox vigorously, warming up; others stare limply into space, energy dormant if not departed. We are reminded of meat. This is flesh on display, on the hook. Some of it black, some white, some Oriental.

The introduction concluded, a young fighter, seconded by a naval man, climbs into the ring and the referee tosses the disk. It falls with the black side up.

Bare-chested and weighed in, VIC observes the black circle from the stage. He clears his throat.

Three teenage GIRLS walk quickly by below.

> BLACK GIRL
Kill him, baby.

> JAPANESE GIRL
He seen me. I gave him this great big smile.

> MEXICAN GIRL
Yeah man, now he'll probably lose.

City College Phone Booth

It is night and the light in the booth is all that illuminates

51

the darkness. VIC is on the phone. His tone correctly suggests long distance.

VIC

No, I won. Yeah wull, it wasn't no great war or nothing. Just kids. *(Then)* Mom okay and everything? How's Jay David? *(Then)* That guy, boy! *(Then)* Yeah wull hell, I just thought it was about time I did, let everybody know where I was anyway. *(Then)* No wull heck, he don't want me to work. He really likes me. Ask Ariel if he ever heard of Curley Mayo.

He opens the booth door and the light goes out. He stares across the dark campus before continuing.

VIC

Well, so anybody call up or anything? *(Then)* I don't know, hell, Janelle or anybody. *(Then)* I know, I know. *(Then)* Hell wull, Connie, this is costing you money so say hello to Mom for me and tell her she can write me care of here, okay? And ask Ariel did he ever hear of Arty Balz who trained this Curley Mayo. And I'll be talking to you, okay?

He hangs up and steps out of the booth. He picks up his valise and heads toward ARTY's.

Street

VIC, in a spirited triumphant run, crosses from the campus to ARTY's house.

Dining Room

ARTY is sitting at the dining-room table with a cup of coffee as VIC enters.

It wasn't it was private or anything. I just didn't want you stuck with the long distance.

ARTY

Could have reversed the charges.

VIC

Hell, right. I didn't think of that.

He starts for his room.

ARTY

(Archly) How is she?

VIC

She's okay. What do you mean?

ARTY

The girlfriend.

VIC

I was calling my sister in Buddy up, Arty.

ARTY

Yeah, that's what you told me.

VIC

You got a beef? What's the matter?

ARTY pushes a folded piece of paper toward VIC.

ARTY

Who's Norris?

VIC

Norise.

ARTY

(Lying) I didn't read it.

53

VIC reads the note and then returns it to the table as though to disclaim it.

> VIC
>
> Hell, I don't even know what she means.

> ARTY
>
> It was sticking in the door when I come in.

VIC picks up the note again and puts it in his pocket.

> VIC
>
> She's just some girl over at school seen me running and we started to talk.

He starts to go.

> ARTY
>
> What does she want?

> VIC
>
> Hell, I only seen her twice. Maybe I told her I'd go to the show or something.

> ARTY
>
> She knows where you live—that's a pretty personal girl.

> VIC
>
> I never told her I'd go to the show. At least not for sure. I mean hell, that's her worry, I forgot.

He exits to the hall and his room.

Bedroom

He turns on the light and drops his bag to the bed. He pulls the radio from it and leans down to plug it in as ARTY comes to the door.

54

You playing square with me, Curley?

VIC

Hell, Arty, do you even have to ask?

ARTY

Do you want to fight or not? That's all I want to know.

VIC

Wull heck, sure, you know I want to fight.

ARTY

Do you think I know anything about fighters?

VIC

Why do they always have to say you're the first time. The first day I met her she comes across and then she tells me I'm the first guy.

ARTY

Did you have her over here in your bed?

VIC grins up at him.

VIC

Oh, you're a bad guy, Arty, the way you talk.

ARTY turns away, blushing.

ARTY

I'll have to listen to myself sometime.

Then grunts desolately and disappears down the hall.

VIC

(Calling after him) You can't even talk without cussing or talking bad, Arty, I'm ashamed of you.

Silence, and VIC's smile fades.

Dining Room

ARTY is back with his coffee cup. In a moment VIC appears
in the hall door, his mood changed.

> VIC
>
> Heck, Arty, I don't know if it's right I'm here with
> you any more or not.

> ARTY
>
> Maybe it's not.

> VIC
>
> Because what am I doing for you?

> ARTY
>
> I ain't asking you to do nothing for me.

> VIC
>
> Yeah, but you're being good to me, and hell I don't
> know.

ARTY looks up.

> ARTY
>
> You know why I'm doing it too.

> VIC
>
> Wull heck, sure I know why.

> ARTY
>
> Why?

> VIC
>
> Wull, ah . . . because you're my buddy.

> ARTY
>
> I'm not your buddy.

VIC

Well, because of why? Because you think I'm Curley
or why?

ARTY

Shit, you know. You don't pull that.

VIC

Yeah, I know why. *(Bitter)* But I'm not going to
talk about it.

He turns and exits down the hall.

Bedroom

VIC comes in and switches on the radio. He takes Norise's
note from his pocket and reads it again. The radio, unfor-
tunately, warms up rather loud.

ARTY appears in the door.

ARTY

And I don't want you playing that fucking radio so
goddamn loud either because I'm not laying around
with sluts all day and I got to get a decent night's
sleep.

VIC takes a step forward and slams the door in ARTY's face.
Now he turns the radio on full blast, and flops on the bed
to stare furiously at the ceiling.

Shortly there is loud knocking on the door. VIC ignores it.
The knocking continues, and ARTY's drowned words from
beyond.

VIC

(Yelling) Cut it out, Arty! Will you leave me alone!

ARTY

It's for you.

VIC

What's for me?

ARTY

The fucking telephone.

VIC jumps to his feet.

VIC

Oh, for me.

Confusion takes over anger and results in a sudden trans-
formation to courtesy.

ARTY

Long distance, I don't know.

ARTY goes down the hall and VIC follows sheepishly, leaving
the radio blaring.

Hallway

He picks up the phone.

VIC

Yeah? Yes, ma'am.

ARTY goes silently into his room at the other end of the hall
and closes the door.

VIC

(*Blushing*) Oh yeah, hi, Janelle, what's doing?
What's going on? This is sure a surprise.

He looks from ARTY's door and the certain eavesdropper
behind it to his own room, where the phone won't reach.

VIC

No, great. Hold on a second, would you?

58

He ducks into the bathroom.

Bathroom

He crouches down to work the cord under the door and then sits on the toilet, clearing his throat manfully before continuing.

> VIC

> Yeah wull, what did she do? Must have called you right up. No, heck, I wanted her to. Yeah wull, what are you doing now, still at the drugstore, or what? *(Then)* No, wull heck, I want you to if it's got to do with me. *(Then)* Oh, yeah? *(Then)* Does he say for sure? Yeah wull, just some doctor in Oakland—how do you know he's any good? *(Then)* Okay, then, I never said he wasn't. So don't go getting all excited, that's all. *(Then)* Sure I do, but what are you getting panicky for? *(Then)* Yes, you are. You're very panicky.

Now ARTY beyond the bathroom door marches loudly from his room to VIC's, where he turns off the radio and then stomps back to his own room and slams the door.

> VIC

> *(Lowers his voice)* Listen, Janelle, I'll call you in a couple of days, okay, and let you know. *(Then)* I can't talk to you now. *(Then)* Okay, then, I won't. *(Then)* Janelle?

He hangs up.

Hallway

VIC comes out of the bathroom. He puts the phone on the stand. He goes into his room.

He listens to the suddenly very still house.

Bedroom

He closes the door. He turns off the light and stands by the window. It is open and tuned to the slick, sinister, unvarying wind of the freeway.

Shortly the shadow of feet appear under the door behind him. There is a faint uncertain knock. When he doesn't answer, the knock is repeated louder.

VIC

Yeah?

ARTY

(*Outside the door*) Did you say yeah?

VIC

Come on in.

The door opens and ARTY comes in.

ARTY

You awake?

The room remains in darkness, so the glare of the hall light intrudes.

ARTY

I got something for you.

VIC

(*Uninterested*) What is it?

ARTY

Curley's robe. (*Silence*) All right if I turn the light on?

He turns on the light and holds up a limp, sweat-stained robe on a hanger.

I'm giving it to you. *(When there is no response)* It's magenda.

You don't want to give me Curley's robe, Arty.

I knew all along I was going to give it to you and now I am.

I'm going to split, Arty. I'm cutting out.

What do you mean?

I'm going home.

Dang it all, yelling at you, is that it?

There's someone there in trouble that shouldn't ought to be and I got to do the right thing.

He goes for his suitcase.

I just been messing around with a lot of phonies down here and trying to be somebody I not even am.

He starts to pack, tears in his eyes.

I'm not who you think I am, Arty.

I know who you are.

VIC

No, you don't.

ARTY

There was no one there tonight you couldn't wipe
out, Curley, and no one I seen in the last ten years.
Are you going to smash that up?

VIC

I don't dig you.

ARTY

Me?

VIC

I understand you but I don't dig your ways.

ARTY

Hell, you mean cussing? Hey, I can stop cussing any
time I want to.

VIC

I never meant to get in this deep.

ARTY

Hell, you're just full of hell . . .

VIC

I just wanted a place to sleep, that's all.

ARTY

Hellaciousness, that's all.

VIC

I ain't got nothing for you, man.

ARTY

Just a hot-blooded kid.

VIC

Well, I'm not going to be that. I'm a cold-blooded kid. The Cold-Blooded Kid.

ARTY

The Cold-Blooded Kid, shit. Bad Boy Peck is all you are. How much does she want?

VIC

And I don't want nobody else's belt and nobody else's robe and nobody else getting me out of my scrapes either. So don't crawl.

ARTY

Crawl?

VIC

Okay then, have it your own way. I don't care. Eat your heart out. But I'm going.

There is sudden silence and he looks up to see what damage his words have done. ARTY stares at him and their eyes lock.

VIC

Aren't you going to say it?

ARTY

Say what?

VIC

You love me.

ARTY

Fuck you, kid.

ARTY BALZ
MANAGER

THIS·IS·IT ·

ONE WAY

U.S.MAIL

THREE

Buddy Gas Station

It is night and hot and bugs as big as bats attack the lights. VIC, wearing a smudged uniform, is in the garage working on a car.

JANELLE is in the office setting up his dinner. She is not visibly pregnant but hopelessness has taken over her former brittle chic and her hair is permanently pincurled for an occasion which does not seem to be arising.

JANELLE
You going to eat or not?

VIC, who has already been called several times, drops his tools and crosses wordlessly to the office. He sits down to a meal too carefully laid out.

VIC
I don't like you to have to come down here all the time, Janelle.

JANELLE

I don't mind.

VIC

Yeah wull, I do.

JANELLE

At least until you know what you plan on doing.

He eats and doesn't answer.

JANELLE

I'll have to fix some Spanish rice sometime.

VIC

Naw, hell, a sandwich is okay.

JANELLE

Most people don't know how to make rice. The real way. Most people it comes out gummy. It should be all separate and firm. That's the way I do it.

At this point a motorcycle pulls up outside.

VIC

Hey, Larken's got his cycle.

Pumps

VIC comes out of the office, followed by JANELLE. LARKEN's motorcycle idles at the pumps, LARKEN and PARKER aboard.

LARKEN

Man, you want to go for a ride?

VIC would like to but JANELLE steps up beside him and takes his arm, tripping as she does so.

74

VIC

Wull hell, I better not, I guess.

PARKER

Go ahead. I'll watch the station.

VIC

I been on a bike before, Parker.

LARKEN

You want to drive out to El Deleria when you close up? *(Making trouble)* Or you busy?

VIC

Hell, Janelle'll do just what I tell her to, won't you, Janelle?

JANELLE stares coldly at these intruders and clings the more firmly to VIC. LARKEN revs his motor.

LARKEN

Well, what do you say? Shall I come back or not?

VIC is happily removed from this tug of war by the arrival of a car at the far side of the station. He departs in that direction.

PARKER

(Uncomfortable) Hey, you quit at the drugstore, huh?

JANELLE

They want me to come back. I may go back, I don't know. *(Lofty and small)* It all depends on Vic.

LARKEN

When are you and Bomber going to get married? I thought you two was going to get married or something.

JANELLE sighs and stares forlornly at VIC, whose customer is a woman, flashy even at this distance.

JANELLE

> I don't know. You'll have to speak to Vic on that. I don't know what his plans are.

Poppy's Car

POPPY, a dark-skinned girl of thirty, used but not soiled, leans from the back seat into the front, where VIC is sprawled, his head under the dash. He is fixing her radio.

POPPY

> It's on in the back now.

VIC

> It's on in the back?

POPPY

> Yeah, but just in the back.

VIC

> Trouble is, it's shorting someplace.

VIC pushes himself farther under and lifts his legs so that they go over into the back seat, one on either side of POPPY.

POPPY

> Now it's on in the front.

Pumps

LARKEN takes off, with PARKER behind.

LARKEN

> See you later, Bealer, okay?

The motorcycle disappears beyond the fluorescence and we see JANELLE return to the station office.

Poppy's Car

> VIC
>
> *(Upside down)* Do you listen to it more in the front or in the back?

> POPPY
>
> Can't you get it in both?

She leans forward, the better to hear, and her head is all but in his crotch.

> POPPY
>
> It's more subtle in the back but if it's something I like I like it in the front too.

VIC twists around to see if JANELLE is watching. She isn't. He looks up at POPPY between his legs.

> VIC
>
> What are you, from up around Tahoe or someplace?

> POPPY
>
> Stateline.

> VIC
>
> Things pretty swinging up there or what?

A car honks for gas and VIC starts.

> VIC
>
> *(To* POPPY*)* Hold on, okay?

Pumps

ROCKOFF and family, which includes LOVETTE and ANDY

JUNIOR, have arrived in their beat-up car. JANELLE is the
first to greet them.

> JANELLE
>
> How are you, Lovette?

> LOVETTE
>
> How are you, Janelle?

> JANELLE
>
> You seen Terilyn Idey lately?

The greater part of JANELLE's interest, however, is with VIC
across the station, untangling himself from POPPY.

> LOVETTE
>
> She quit her job at the dairy, I know. You seen Van-
> dell?

> JANELLE
>
> She's trying to get my old job at the drugstore.

> LOVETTE
>
> That Vandell.

> JANELLE
>
> That Terilyn.

> LOVETTE
>
> She'd try anything.

JANELLE crouches down to see into the back seat, where a
baby overflows from a hanging swing.

> JANELLE
>
> How are you, Andy Junior?

> LOVETTE
>
> Don't get him started.

ROCKOFF honks again, comically, he thinks, as VIC approaches.

ROCKOFF

Hey, what do you do around here for service?

VIC

Hey, Fatso, what's happening?

LOVETTE

We just stopped by to see what you guys was going to do.

ROCKOFF

What time do you get off, Bomber? Why'n cha come over for a beer?

VIC

Why don't you go over with Lovette, Janelle, and I'll close up.

JANELLE

(Worried) I don't mind waiting.

VIC

Just see Rockoff don't drink up all the beer before I get there.

He opens the back seat for her.

LOVETTE

He would, too.

JANELLE

You going to come right over or what?

She looks anxiously toward POPPY.

ROCKOFF

Boy oh boy, you two are worse off than we are and you're not even married.

LOVETTE

Andy, I'm going to slap you.

JANELLE

You're not going out to El Deleria—?

VIC

Do you mind just doing what I ask you to, dumb-head?

JANELLE gets in the car and slams the door. The moment is uncomfortable for everyone. LOVETTE punches ROCKOFF to get on the way.

ROCKOFF

See you later, sport, okay?

VIC watches the group depart as a police car races down the highway, its sirens screaming. A moment later an ambulance follows as VIC crosses back to POPPY.

Poppy's Car

She waits for him in the passenger seat.

VIC

Well, what did you decide? Do you want it in the front or in the back?

Pumps

A short time has passed. Though still open, the station seems deserted. The lights are blazing and the bugs in action, but VIC is not in sight.

A car waits for service and a MAN beside it honks his horn. No one appears. The MAN crosses toward the office.

Hey, anybody here?

VIC comes from behind the station, fastening his pants and
sticking in his shirttail.

MAN

I was wondering where everybody was.

VIC

(Rattled) Fill her up?

MAN

I didn't know if someone was here or if you'd all
took off down to see the wreck.

VIC

What'd they have a wreck?

VIC puts a hose to the MAN's car.

MAN

Couple kids on a motorbike rammed into a stalled
truck.

VIC

Hey, no. Heck. Hey.

MAN

One of them they found a half mile away without so
much as a scratch, wandering around in a daze. But
cut the other one's head clean off.

Buddy County Cemetery

VIC stands with JANELLE apart from the other mourners
some distance from the grave. A pathetic wail that began in
the previous scene now fades as MRS. LARKEN is led away by
friends and the other mourners disperse. Among these are

ROCKOFF and LOVETTE, who help PARKER, on crutches in an ankle cast.

                    VIC
Oh, yeah, make a lot of noise over the grave . . .

                    JANELLE
Vic . . .

                    VIC
He appreciates that.

                    JANELLE
Come on, honey.

                    VIC
What did they ever do for him when he was alive?

                    JANELLE
Let's go for a walk until they're gone.

She takes his arm and guides him toward the back regions of the cemetery.

                    VIC
Put up some crappy thing: here lies Larken. Beloved of no one. *Thee* end.

Elsewhere in the Cemetery

Here the gravestones are uncommon and contemporary in design, though very old and overgrown with plants and vines, in some cases heavy-laden with grapes. A few markers are cylindrical and so bluntly phallic as to seem someone's joke. The inscriptions are Oriental.

                    VIC
They had Chinese once in Buddy. Only now I guess they all died.

He stands gloomily awe-struck at his own words and the exotic upthrust stones around him.

VIC

> Look at all them I guess Chinese.

JANELLE sinks to a small stone wall, tired of small talk, however weighty.

VIC

> And now nobody even thinks of them.

JANELLE

> Nobody thinks of nobody.

VIC

> Just stick them out here and then forget.

Turning in a slow complete circle, he surveys the countryside. Under the trees here it is cool, but all around stretch hot fields and dusty roads.

VIC

> I bet there ain't a Chinese now in any direction.

JANELLE

> I told my father, Vic.

VIC

> Yeah?

JANELLE

> He was mad I wasn't working and he said what did I plan on doing, sit on my can all day. So I just got mad and screamed at him leave me alone.

VIC

> Wull hell, he better not come gunning after me.

JANELLE

> He won't.

VIC

Because he never done anything for you, so he better not try and give me hell.

JANELLE

He said he'd give me four hundred dollars.

VIC

Hell, I'm not going to take his money.

JANELLE

What am I supposed to do, Vic, then?

VIC

What's he want you to?

JANELLE

To go to my real mother's in El Paso and he'll give me four hundred dollars. She's a nurse and maybe she'll know someone if it's not too late.

VIC

How come he don't want us to get married?

JANELLE

(Moistly) He cares something for me. How I feel. It's obvious you're not in any hurry and—well, I am. Lovette already knows just by looking at me and if I wait any too much longer everybody in town will.

VIC frowns fiercely at the countryside.

VIC

Oh crap, I hate this place. I hate Buddy. I wish it was all out here underground.

JANELLE looks at him. His answer is anger and that is no answer. But she expected nothing more.

84

JANELLE

You'll be free and I'll be free.

VIC

No, heck, I don't want you to have to do that to
yourself, Janelle.

She waits to hear his alternative.

VIC

(Finally) Yeah wull, you just tell your old man I'm
going to imburse him every penny, that's all.

JANELLE

You don't have to do that.

VIC

You just tell him that, every goddamn nickel.

JANELLE

He's doing it for me, not for you. My father cares
what people say about me, Vic.

VIC sighs. He touches her pointlessly. Apology is all the love
he has.

VIC

Some summer, huh?

FOUR

San Francisco Civic Auditorium

Along the inner balcony of this building is a sign which identifies the present event as the 1963 San Francisco Examiner Golden Gloves and Pacific Association A.A.U. Boxing Championships.

VIC is in the ring, matched with a strong black fighter. It's the last fight of the evening and we stay with it for the full three rounds, for the first time seeing VIC in action. One thing is clear, he has the qualities of strength and concentration which make the good boxer; added to which is that modesty of the masterful that gives to his victories the becoming touch of embarrassment.

VIC has the advantage. Black girls in the audience scream abuse. Which offends the faithful RODINE at ringside, who rolls her eyes to NOLA, as though to say what more can you expect of the lower classes.

Next to NOLA, a seemingly proper GENTLEMAN volunteers:

87

I follow these boys. They're wonderful boys. I follow them wherever they go. It's my whole life. I'm their number-one fan. Will you be going to the Nationals? I will.

NOLA leans closer, the better to hear this stranger. Her eyes fall to his lap, where under a natty topcoat spread across his knees, he vigorously masturbates.

NOLA straightens. Shortly, she nudges RODINE. Who moves forward to look and then taps BETT on the back. BETT is in the row ahead. RODINE whispers in her ear.

BETT turns wide-eyed to stare at the veiled industry in the lap behind her. She squints and blinks and seems to sniff before turning forward again. She leans against CONNIE on her right and passes the news on.

CONNIE turns with no attempt to conceal her interest. She stares. Her mouth falls open. Suddenly blushing she turns around again and reaches for JAY DAVID's ear. His eyes widen.

JAY DAVID

Where?

In the ring the referee breaks up a clinch. The crowd reacts negatively. VIC looks to his corner for direction, but ARIEL, out of his depth in the big time, is too anxious even to root. Others in these sidelines we recognize from Buddy are: PARKER, with a camera, ROCKOFF and LOVETTE, and the uniformed High School Drill Team, starring as majorette the now-matured and overly pretty DRENNA VALENTINE.

In the end VIC gets a split decision and, stricken with this accomplishment and what it took to get it and sweaty and swathed in towels, he is escorted from the ring to the dressing room by an eager crowd of family and home-town followers touching glory in his trail now and nevermore.

JAY DAVID rallies the Drill Team into formation.

RODINE retrieves SHEREEN from the dressing room where the child studies half-naked boxers with trussed genitalia.

> SHEREEN
> Why is that man wearing a bandage?

> RODINE
> Can't you let anyone have any privacy, Shereen?

She drags her daughter out, collecting hairy butt and murky groin herself with wistful backward glance.

> RODINE
> People don't want you staring at them getting dressed. You know better than that.

Coming from the showers, VIC parts a cluster of clinging boys who taunt and flatter in the same breath. They follow him down the hall, leaving behind in sudden quiet the untended fighter VIC beat.

Meanwhile in the foyer of the auditorium, littered with discarded programs and empty popcorn boxes, JAY DAVID rehearses the Drill Team.

> JAY DAVID
> Nice squad, nice squad, left right, left. Right left, right kick, about left, right. Left right, left right, left right, lean. Nice squad, nice squad, nice squad, cheer.

The cheer is faint and embarrassed as indifferent stragglers wander through the formation and push out into the night.

Elsewhere in the hall, where friends and family of other

fighters wait, NOLA, CONNIE, RODINE, BETT, PARKER, ROCKOFF and LOVETTE are clustered along marble steps. SHEREEN hangs upside down from the banister.

VIC comes from the dressing room, ARIEL with him. He carries his trophy and seeing his gang waiting he holds it triumphantly high.

They charge toward him with a forced scream, at the last moment standing back to give NOLA the primary position. And she who subscribes to the thesis that between the practical and the demonstrative the former is the deeper love, instead of kissing him as everyone is anxious to do, reaches up to inspect the cut above his bruised and puffy eye. To NOLA, motherhood has this rule: play it down.

> NOLA
> Shouldn't he have some stitches in that before it opens up again?

> VIC
> Heck no.

> ARIEL
> I want to be able to watch it . . .

> VIC
> Stitches will make a scar.

> ARIEL
> . . . don't get soft underneath with the State Wide coming up.

> VIC
> You don't think I want to end up looking like Ariel, do you?

> CONNIE
> With that ugly puss you got, a few scars ain't going to hurt.

She kisses him.

Marlon's afraid the girls won't go for him if he gets
all beat up.

She kisses him too.

Next in line is RODINE, to whom VIC surrenders his trophy
rather than be kissed. Her infatuation is that manic and
dampening.

Hey, Parker, you going to get my picture in the Bee?

The Drill Team marches around the corner and, to the
chagrin of any serious Golden Glovers left, chants:

DRILL TEAM

V-I-C-B, V-I-C-B,
E-A-L, E-A-L,
E-R! E-R! E-R!

They engulf the Buddy gang, VIC red-faced and seething
until they move on and disperse.

JAY DAVID turns up in their wake.

JAY DAVID

(Eager to be appreciated) How does that make you
feel, Bomber? Pretty great, huh?

VIC

Why did you have to go and do that, J.D.?

JAY DAVID

What's the matter?

VIC

Bring all them kids for.

JAY DAVID

I?

CONNIE

The whole senior class, Vic, showed up.

JAY DAVID

Fans don't hurt, Bomber.

ARIEL

It's a bad deal, Jay—home-town stuff.

CONNIE

Don't hurt nobody to know he's popular with his own that I can see.

JAY DAVID

You got to get used to having fans around, Bomber. That's part of the game.

VIC

(Wincing) The game.

ARIEL

We don't want to look small-time, J.D., is all.

There is a silence heaped with embarrassment, anger and guilt.

VIC

Wull heck, what are we all just standing around for?

NOLA

You going to drive back with us?

VIC

Wull heck, I come with Ariel and Bett.

ARIEL

Hell, you go with them. We're out back.

92

CONNIE

Jay David rent a bus for all the Buddy people, Vic.

ARIEL holds his ground, BETT beside him.

ARIEL

I'm beat anyway. You go on. I been feeling lousy.

VIC

(A false discomfort) Yeah, but we was going to have a drink or something, weren't we, hell.

CONNIE, JAY DAVID, RODINE and SHEREEN drift toward the front door; NOLA, too.

ARIEL

You and me can have a drink any time, Bomber. You go on.

VIC

Well, I guess I should kind of ought to go with Mom, okay, Arie?

He backs guiltily toward his family.

ARIEL

Just remember, don't let tonight go to your head. You're still a working man and I expect to see you at six-thirty tomorrow same as any other day.

ARIEL and BETT watch the group depart down the long hall. BETT plants a consoling smack on her husband's cheek, and ARIEL touches his heart uneasily. Then they exit out the back.

Auditorium Exterior, Night

The Drill Team and other Buddians climb on board the bus parked at the curb. NOLA once more inspects VIC's brow, CONNIE and JAY DAVID flanking her.

NOLA

I don't like the looks of this, J.D., soft underneath
or not.

VIC

Lay off, it's okay.

He looks around craftily.

NOLA

All swolled up.

VIC

Maybe I should go with Ariel, Mom.

JAY DAVID

(Anxious) I wanted to have a little talk with you,
Vic, if I my.

VIC

Hell, he's worked pretty hard for me tonight and
maybe I should better kind of go have a drink with
him or something.

CONNIE

Jay David's been looking forward to talking to you
about something, Vic.

NOLA

Let the boy suit himself.

All epaulets and gold buttons, DRENNA VALENTINE pushes
past to get on the bus.

DRENNA

How are you, Mrs. Bealer?

JAY DAVID

What do you hear from your daddy, Drenna, still
liking Europe?

DRENNA

I guess so. How are you, Vic?

JAY DAVID

Next time you tell them they can send me.

DRENNA

(To VIC) Shall I save a seat for you?

VIC shrugs and DRENNA reads acquiescence. She disappears into the bus.

VIC

Who's that?

NOLA

You know Drenna Valentine, Vic.

JAY DAVID

I told High the next time he wants to go to Europe he should send me.

VIC

I guess I just never seen her grown up.

CONNIE

You call that grown up?

JAY DAVID

He means with all that money. *(Getting things going)* All aboard.

But VIC withdraws.

VIC

I'll come out to the stockyards tomorrow, J.D., and see you then, okay?

It's a disappointment he's not coming, but before they can protest further, VIC kisses first CONNIE and then NOLA on the cheek.

Third in line, JAY DAVID steps back and extends his hand, chuckling embarrassedly.

> JAY DAVID
> Just a formal handshake will do for me, thanks.

He clutches JAY DAVID's hand and then departs.

NOLA, CONNIE, JAY DAVID (and from inside the bus, DRENNA) watch VIC trot amiably away, long accustomed to the feeling of letdown their love for him entails.

Auditorium

An old man with an umbrella under his arm reacts as VIC enters this vast deserted hall. Mumbling dates and giving out shattered facts about his past, he breaks into a vague soft shoe and shuffles after VIC through the litter and waste of the slick reflecting floor.

But VIC ignores him and continues on his way among the empty chairs.

Rear Auditorium Exterior

VIC comes out. He surveys the ground before he bounds down the steps and heads for the last car remaining in the parking lot.

Car

He looks around first to see that everyone is gone. Then he gets into the car.

POPPY is behind the wheel.

POPPY

(After a moment) What do you want to do?

VIC shrugs.

POPPY

Hungry?

VIC

Sure.

POPPY

Want to eat something?

VIC

I don't want to eat nothing I can't eat lying down.

POPPY starts the car.

Stairs to Coit Tower, Dawn

VIC and POPPY climb the endless zigzag of wooden stairs that scale the rear of Russian Hill, their voices fading in.

POPPY

This guy I knew in Hawaii? I mean he had lots of money. He was a surfer but he broke his neck. So he went over to England, you know, where they used to have the marches against the war. He was marching before anyone was marching and he got put in jail and everyone in his family was all embarrassed. He wasn't a drag or anything. Yeah, he was a drag, but he didn't mean no harm. He was just for everybody. He was kind of a drag. And then he flipped out in jail and nobody knows whatever became of him.

They have stopped briefly to get their breath.

> VIC
>
> Did he lay you?

> POPPY
>
> You mean before he went to England?

> VIC
>
> Yeah, or after.

> POPPY
>
> I don't think after. Maybe before. No, maybe after.

VIC resumes the climb and POPPY follows.

> POPPY
>
> His name was Wesley and he was from Baltimore and the girl he was engaged to was Catholic and without no conscience and was really dragged he was a surfer and really dragged when he started marching. Is something the matter?

> VIC
>
> You don't even remember if he scored on you.

> POPPY
>
> Hey, don't put me down, daddy. There's a lot to remember and none of it half as interesting as you all'd like to think.

VIC sulks as they cross a street and ascend more stairs.

> POPPY
>
> I told you I was a Celebrity Screwer.

> VIC
>
> I'll break your back if you say that again.

POPPY

I laid James Dean.

VIC

The heck, Poppy, you never did.

POPPY

My girlfriend did. She told me.

VIC

That's not you.

POPPY

I would if he weren't dead.

VIC

You're so phony.

POPPY

She works in Las Vegas and she just goes into the
dressing room and says if you got five minutes here
it is.

VIC

Boy, Poppy, you make me shudder.

They reach the next level and start up a steep street.

POPPY

Some people they get everything handed to them,
and then, boy, some of the things I've heard about
some of these guys.

VIC

What guys?

POPPY

You read all about those Hollywood guys getting in
trouble and taking dope and things.

99

VIC

I'd never take any dope. That's one thing I've decided.

POPPY

And hanging themselves, and for what?

VIC

It's not any all roses being somebody.

POPPY

They're all just trying to wreck their careers.

VIC

What, do you personally know some Hollywood person?

POPPY

I'm not ashamed to say it, I like people who are some-
bodies.

VIC

I guess James Dean smashed up his career.

POPPY

Just give me a chance and you won't see me ruining
it.

VIC

Because one thing I wouldn't even do is let anyone
even in my dressing room.

POPPY has to run to catch up.

POPPY

Except, no, you want to have something to remember, don't you?

VIC

Because I belong to me.

He grants another short pause in their climb.

VIC

You know this Ariel I told you about?

POPPY

Who's Ariel, your girlfriend?

VIC

He's my trainer.

POPPY

Oh, trainer.

VIC

Everything I need—my manager, my cut man, my matchmaker, my friend . . .

He continues upward now and POPPY pulls herself along.

POPPY

Seems like everybody up there is just trying to ruin themselves.

VIC

Well, you know his wife? She's all the time saying how I look like Marlon Brando.

POPPY

I don't see that.

VIC

Hell, I don't look like Marlon Brando.

POPPY

All Marlon Brando would ever have to do is just ask me and I would.

I wasn't just kidding, Poppy. I'll break your back
you talk that way in front of me.

Coit Tower

They cross the empty parking lot toward POPPY's car. The
street is damp with dawn.

POPPY

Because when you think of Marilyn Monroe for in-
stance, what are you supposed to think?

VIC

What?

POPPY

Is it unworthy or what?

VIC

I don't know.

POPPY

Or meanness or what to have something beautiful
and hold out. That everybody else would die to
have and you got to throw it away. But I guess you
got to have the stomach for it.

VIC

I liked Marilyn.

POPPY

Everybody did.

VIC

But I guess that's what you got to have, the stomach
for it.

POPPY

Nobody likes to see nobody throw themselves down the drain like that I guess.

VIC stands on the wall before POPPY's car and surveys the morning panorama of cloud and bay and smoldering industry.

VIC

Hell, but show me somebody that don't throw themselves down the drain.

POPPY

Most people don't kill themselves, though.

VIC

Do you know that over ninety percent of the population of America goes to work at a job they hate?

POPPY tidies up the back seat of her car. This is where they spent the night.

POPPY

They're blue but they don't kill themselves. They sit in a bar or mess up, but they don't commit suicide.

VIC

Just put in a harness to make the pull with everyone else. That's down the drain, only slow.

He sits down on the wall. POPPY joins him.

VIC

It's not that I'm so great but—

POPPY

You're beautiful.

VIC

Yeah, maybe I am beautiful. Sometimes I think I am. And that's why I don't let anybody get a piece of me.

POPPY

I did.

VIC

Because they think they can buy anybody.

POPPY

Who?

VIC

Oh, anybody. I ain't saying I'm holding out because who will, but I just don't see any reason, that's all. I mean, hell, I just don't want anything they got, that's all. Anybody, I mean. What they got is lousy.

POPPY

Most people they don't even have a conscience.

VIC

Actually I don't see no reason to do nothing. I'm just not interested.

POPPY regards him sadly, not comprehending such self-denial.

POPPY

But don't you want to have something to remember?

VIC

You're so phony, Poppy.

He starts for the car.

104

No, they're beautiful and I want to give myself to them and I don't see nothing wrong in that.

VIC gets in the car.

POPPY

(Alone with her philosophy) Because if they'd only just appreciate how beautiful they were, then maybe they wouldn't all have to hang themselves and crack up.

Stockyards

VIC sits high on the timbers of a corral as JAY DAVID runs stock through the slaughter-house pens.

JAY DAVID

Well, Vic, it's real clear to everybody that you got the makings of a boxer. I mean it's clear to everybody that you're a real strong boy.

VIC

Not if I don't start getting to bed.

JAY DAVID

And like last night you proved to everybody that it'll be nothing to take the West Coast title and probably after that the Nationals real easy. So here's what I'd like to do. Well, I don't want to rush you, but just think about it. Hell, there's no reason to rush. You got your whole life in front of you. And I appreciate the sport of it and all. After all, how many Fights of the Week have me and you watched together anyway?

What are you talking about, J.D.?

Well, I asked Connie if she thought it would be all right if I talked to you and she said she thought it would be all right. After all, all he can do is throw that left at you . . .

He ducks comically, though no left is thrown.

And I said what left . . .?

He chuckles forcedly and without effect.

So, no, I'd like you to think about it. Not tomorrow or the next day. Wait until after the finals if you want to, or if you want the Olympics, if they mean so damn much to you. But how old are you, Vic, getting to be?

Okay, I'm not any kid.

You know you're not any kid any more is what I'm saying.

Tempest Fugit.

No, there's a lot of truth in that.

What are you driving at, J.D.?

JAY DAVID

Not that you're old or anything.

VIC

Hell, man, I'm really beat. What are you getting to?
I been up all night.

JAY DAVID

Hell, maybe you'll never turn pro, I don't know.
But what I mean is, if you did . . . I mean you
wouldn't sign nothing with nobody else, would you?
(Silence) I know that Ariel knows a lot about boxing and there's a lot that I don't know about boxing—

VIC

You don't know a damn thing about boxing, Jay.

JAY DAVID

Well, that's why I brought it up was because I
wanted you to know I'm prepared to quit out here
whenever you're ready to make the big decision and
get behind you one hundred percent and give you
my whole time to working for you. *(Silence)* What
I'm saying is, for the sake of keeping it in the family,
I'm prepared . . . and after all, out here's been my
bread and butter . . . and I guess you know you're
going to be a uncle again by the way . . . and your
mother living with us, Vic . . . I've never men-
tioned this but the payments on Larry's house for
Rodine and the kids . . .

VIC sighs bitterly.

JAY DAVID

The way I put it to Connie was that you need someone behind you to protect you from all these guys—

107

                              VIC
What guys, J.D.?

                          JAY DAVID
Oh, after last night believe me there's going to be
guys around you and they're going to be after something. They seen you got fans.

                              VIC
You're something else, J.D.

                          JAY DAVID
But to someone in your own family it's different
Someone in your own family is going to look out for
you and what I'm saying is I'm prepared to make
the sacrifice out here.

VIC wipes dust from his mouth. He looks at the wide-eyed,
anxious cattle, the coughing sheep crowding the fence.

                          JAY DAVID
Well, what are you thinking, Bomber? We're not all
the strong silent types, you know. Some of us need a
few words of encouragement to know where we
stand.

VIC jumps down into the corral.

                              VIC
I just wish you hadn't opened your mouth, Jay
David. Goddamn you.

                          JAY DAVID
Oh?

                              VIC
I just wish you could have kept all that crap inside
yourself. But you couldn't, could you?

Sure I can, Vic, hell.

But VIC walks away through the bleating livestock.

Dock

A stockyard WORKER loads the open trunk of DRENNA's sports car with a box of frozen meat as DRENNA stands by watching VIC's brooding departure down a dirt road that exits the stockyards on the far side.

The WORKER closes the trunk.

> WORKER
>
> You hurry home before all this gets unfroze now.

DRENNA drives off as a gloomy JAY DAVID arrives at the dock. He stares after her.

In the distance her car stops beside VIC. When the dust has cleared, JAY DAVID and the WORKER see DRENNA scoot over and VIC get in behind the wheel.

> WORKER
>
> That meat's going to spoil if she don't take it right home.

Vic's Mountain

VIC is in the driver's seat of DRENNA's car, and DRENNA, beside him, reclines against the passenger door, a loose safety belt strapped across her torso. They are parked on an incline that surveys the vast valley soft in the powdery light of late afternoon.

VIC removes his shirt and wipes the sweat from his chest. He smells the shirt, then throws it in the back. He pretends to relax. They have nothing in common, these two, and the silence is prolonged and heavy.

VIC

You know how long since I been to sleep?

DRENNA

I like it up here.

VIC

Oh, man, if this place could talk.

His tired eyes smile out over the still distance.

DRENNA

The stories it could tell, I suppose.

VIC

The stories it could tell.

DRENNA

Couldn't you get to sleep last night? All the excitement, I suppose.

VIC

You know what my record is for non-sleep? Three days once when Larry come to L.A.

DRENNA

Did you ever bring Janelle Sharkey up here?

VIC

Naw, hell, you don't bring no girls up here you're serious about, just pigs. *(Then)* Except, no, it's all right in the daytime.

DRENNA

Shall I turn on the radio?

VIC

It's your car.

DRENNA

Oh, Vic . . . you have such a sense of humor.

She turns on the radio.

VIC

Well, that's all I got. I ain't telling you no different.

DRENNA

You'll have whatever you want some day.

VIC

Yeah, I know I will.

DRENNA

Because I'm sure of that.

VIC

Hell, I'm sure of it too.

DRENNA

Dieu est avec vous.

VIC

Only I won't just have it tomorrow or by next Friday is what I'm saying.

DRENNA

Anyone that loves you is willing to wait.

VIC

You mean my mother or what?

DRENNA

Your mother and those people who believe in you.

VIC

Don't believe in me.

DRENNA

Le succès est le vôtre.

VIC

First thing I better do is go back to school.

DRENNA

It's French.

VIC

Your people in Europe or what?

DRENNA

They're coming home.

VIC

What is your dad, a major or what? In the army?

DRENNA

What do you hear from Janelle?

VIC

Sharkey?

DRENNA

She still in El Paso?

VIC

Far as I know. You a friend of Janelle's?

DRENNA

I didn't know if you were still going together or what.

VIC

I don't go with no one.

DRENNA

That's what I told Terilyn Idey, that Rockoff was just nothing but a big liar.

112

VIC

Rockoff?

DRENNA

I don't go with nobody either.

VIC

How do you mean Rockoff is a big liar?

DRENNA

I think going with people is asinine.

VIC

Do you know Rockoff?

DRENNA

You see people going with people and they're just
standing still.

VIC

What's eating Rockoff? What's he trying to pull?

DRENNA

He's just saying Lovette's getting all these letters
from Janelle, that's all.

VIC

Lots of people get letters.

DRENNA

That's exactly what I told Terilyn Idey.

VIC

What is?

DRENNA

That it was all probably just lies.

VIC

Wull, what is?

DRENNA

I don't gossip, Vic.

VIC

What is she, having a real ball down there, I suppose.

DRENNA

Who?

VIC

Janelle.

DRENNA

Where?

VIC

In El Paso.

DRENNA

She's in L.A.

VIC

L.A.?

DRENNA

For one thing, Rockoff can be glad you don't know what he's saying or you'd knock his block clear off if I know you.

VIC

What's Rockoff trying to pull, Drenna? Are you my friend or not?

DRENNA

It just makes me sick because what business is it of everybody's even if Janelle did have a baby and you tried to say it wasn't yours?

VIC says nothing. He stares into the valley at a car speeding along the distant road.

DRENNA

Because if she don't care enough about you to write you that she's down in L.A. when she's writing everyone in town and telling them she's married some creep down there and made a record and everything—

VIC

Made a record?

DRENNA

Yeah, she went to L.A. and made a record, Vic, and somebody's got to tell you.

VIC

Yeah?

DRENNA

So what are you supposed to do, Vic, honestly? I don't blame you. And as far as I'm concerned she really messed up and missed out on something really great last night. Because you're a thousand times better than any Janelle Sharkey. Because I still can't get my breath.

VIC's look has turned to a vague bitter smile.

DRENNA

What are you thinking?

VIC

I ain't thinking nothing.

DRENNA

A person is always thinking something.

VIC

Not me.

115

Sometimes they might not know it but they have always got something on their minds going on.

VIC

This didn't always used to be a cruddy place. Or maybe it always was. Used to when I was a kid, me and Lare if we was going to hike somewhere, this is where we did.

DRENNA

I can always tell when you got something on your mind.

VIC

I guess it was always a pretty cruddy place. Used to we'd always find rubbers a lot.

DRENNA

I like it up here.

VIC

Don't see them so much no more.

El Deleria

This is a crossroads tavern, popular without being prosperous and loud with pinball bells and Mexican music. VIC at one end of the short bar has just hit ROCKOFF and sent him sprawling back through the tables. The others present, mostly farm workers and hefty women, stare but do not move. Except for PARKER, who is immediately on his feet.

PARKER

Jesus, Bealer, what's the matter with you? Why did you do that?

VIC is drunk, dazed and dangerous.

I told you I was going to do something.

PARKER sees the bartender calling the police.

PARKER

Come on, let's get out of here.

VIC

Hell, it'll take the cops an hour to get out here from town. What's the hurry?

He returns to his seat at the bar.

VIC

Let's have a beer.

Vic's Mountain, Night

Ordinarily at night from this spot one sees nothing but the stars overhead, an occasional pair of headlights along the back roads below and in the distance the faint modest twinkle of Buddy. Now, however, the flashing red light of a police car is seen racing along the floor of the valley, and distantly its siren can be heard.

But the three men in ROCKOFF's car pay no attention.

The car is dark. A pair of feet are propped in an open window. The radio plays. We see a glow of a cigarette and a beer can flies out and lands in the dirt.

VIC

I just knew I was going to do it, that's all. Sometimes I just know I'm going to do something.

ROCKOFF

(Thickly) Yeah, but hell, man, why me?

VIC

Move your anatomy, will you, I got to take a leak.

The car door opens and VIC all but crawls out. He takes a few woozy steps in the dark and then unzips his fly.

VIC

Hey, did you read about that disc jockey who in New York or someplace for some disease didn't sleep for how long was it? I got him beat by—

A hand clutches his shoulder. Continuing to urinate, VIC turns vaguely to see who it is. It is ROCKOFF, who pulls him around and slams a fist into his face.

ROCKOFF

Hey, you pissed on me. He pissed on me.

He holds his clammy pants leg tragically as VIC gets unsteadily to his feet and returns the blow. Halfhearted, drunk, exhausted, they continue to besiege one another until each is unconscious or dead in the dark.

Buddy Boys' Club

It's the next day and VIC, hung over and badly scratched and bruised, leans back against the barbells of this makeshift gym as ARIEL concernedly doctors his eye, previously injured and now critical. BETT supervises, steaming.

VIC

He's all the time trying to give me a bad time. They're all just saying, when are you going to get married, Vic, when are you going to settle down. And jeeze, they'd all just give anything to be me. Going around places, just cutting out—

118

BETT

You're so dumb, Vic.

ARIEL

Never mind, Bett.

BETT

All Andy Rockoff wants to say is he beat up Vic Bealer, and you fell for that.

VIC

Yeah wull, he don't get to say that yet.

ARIEL

(To BETT, *defensive)* Anybody gets a few beers in him and all he wants to do is fool around, that's normal.

VIC

And all they are is strapped and married to some girl they had to.

He winces and pulls away.

ARIEL

That hurt?

VIC

Naw, hell, it ain't nothing. I can probably still fight.

BETT

You won't be fighting for months, Bomber, with that.

ARIEL

Didn't I tell you never mind, Bett?

BETT

Even if Ariel'd let you, no ring doctor would.

ARIEL

(Darkly) It looks pretty opened up, Vic, I don't know . . .

VIC

Then I guess there's no point in holding this out . . .

He raises a swollen hand in the air.

VIC

. . . it's broke.

He glares at them, defying them to criticize

VIC

I guess there goes the finals, huh, is that what you're saying?

BETT

There goes everything.

ARIEL

Skip it, will you, Bett.

BETT

No, I'm going to talk to Marlon and afterwards he don't have to talk to me because maybe I won't be talking to him.

VIC

Hell, I'm not just going to stand there and let my name be smirched.

BETT

I'll tell you what your name is—mud around here.

VIC

Because his own mother-in-law caught him laying his wife's sister and his wife caught him laying the fifteen-year-old baby-sitter. So what's he talking about me for all over town is what I'd like to know.

ARIEL sourly opens a bottle of Pepto-Bismol. He pours some into a spoon.

> ARIEL
>
> What Bett's saying, Vic, is you got to learn how to be bigger than the circumstances that come along, that's all.

He gulps down his medicine.

> BETT
>
> What I'm saying is you're letting everybody down, Bomber.

> VIC
>
> She told me she was going to have a bortion.

> BETT
>
> Then how can you believe anything she says?

> VIC
>
> I don't want you to bother me, Bett. I know how you feel, so shut up. Or Ariel either.

He gets to his feet.

> BETT
>
> You're not going to be nothing but a jerk down there.

> VIC
>
> No, if I got some little kid of mine walking around . . .

> BETT
>
> She doesn't need you now, Marlon.

What I'm saying, Vic, is you don't got any too many
more chances any more.

VIC heads for the door.

You'll find someone, Arie.

Come on now, Bomber, let's take a look at that
hand.

Someday some kid's going to walk in here and you'll
really love him and he'll really be great and he
won't let you down.

Hell, come on now, we're just having one of our
heart-to-hearts, Vic—

So I'll just be seeing you, okay?

Nodding with bitter, righteous satisfaction he exits.

BETT bites her lip and looks at ARIEL, who pulls the ring
rope taut and then releases it.

FIVE

Pershing Square, Los Angeles

VIC, in white Levi's and T-shirt, sits on a pipe fence that borders the park walkway. His hand is taped. At his feet is the familiar plaid plastic suitcase.

Nearby several homosexuals are clustered—Latins, blacks and whites, bleached and mascaraed and one at least fur-coated. They eye VIC good-humoredly and he nods awkwardly back and looks elsewhere; and shortly eases himself off the fence and takes up his suitcase and moves.

Toward a woman PREACHER swollen with her calling and buoyantly rocking back and forth on her heels as she witnesses to an indifferent crowd, her voice vibrant and piercing if lacking persuasion.

> PREACHER
>
> For who am I? I am nothing. And I know I am nothing.

She clutches a Bible to her waist, an oddly dainty gravity, and VIC, a figure of health and beauty and youth amid the vagrant, the deviant, the old and unwell and the crazed, is transfixed. For if, as we know, he lacks innocence, he's the deeper believer for it; more the fanatic and hungry for grace.

> PREACHER
> And though there was a day when I thought I was something, when I thought I could walk in anywhere with all my fancy cars and jewels and businesses and bank accounts—there was one place I could not get in, despite a beauty parlor combed my hair twice a day.

VIC swallows hard, conversion imminent.

> PREACHER
> And that place is heaven. Are you ready?

Nursery in the Dearly Home

A night-light illuminates VIC who stares down into the crib of a sleeping infant. He clears his throat and turns to the hall, as though fearing to be caught at this vigil.

A toilet flushes and a naked figure passes the door. VIC withdraws.

Hallway

He moves on tiptoe down the hall.

Master Bedroom

VIC comes in as JANELLE is struggling anxiously into her housecoat.

124

JANELLE

Oh, you scared me. I thought you were gone.

VIC

I was in the little boy's room.

JANELLE

Where?

VIC

Nothing. I was just in the can.

JANELLE

I was in the john, what do you mean?

VIC

I was just looking at the kid. Is that all right?

JANELLE

How come you got dressed?

VIC

Yeah wull, I thought I'd get dressed.

JANELLE

I was just brushing my teeth. You want coffee or anything?

VIC

Naw, heck, I better get going.

He crosses to the window and pulls back the drapes. The glass is streaked with rain.

JANELLE

The buses don't start until six.

VIC

I can walk.

JANELLE

(Scoffing) You'll walk.

VIC

I can hitch a ride. Just show me which way the freeway is.

JANELLE

In that?

She joins him at the window. The rain is formidable.

JANELLE

You could stay.

VIC

Yeah, and when what's-his-name comes home, what
do I do, just move over?

JANELLE

He's at National Guard. He won't be coming home.

VIC

Wull hell, think, woman. Why didn't you get the
car? You could drive me.

JANELLE

He doesn't trust me with the car. He thinks I play
around.

VIC

Yeah, wull heck, I better get going.

He moves away from her.

JANELLE

I'm not holding you.

VIC

Did I put my suitcase somewhere?

JANELLE

Do you want cab fare?

VIC

Yeah, wull okay, I'll have a cup of coffee if it's so important.

Kitchen

VIC sits at the table. Under a low work light, JANELLE moves from counter to sink to icebox, preparing a tray.

JANELLE

(Finally) I wish you'd stop chattering, Vic. It's getting on my nerves.

VIC

Yeah wull, what about you?

JANELLE

I'm afraid of anything I might say.

VIC

Go on, talk. I probably won't understand it anyway.

JANELLE

Or pretend not to.

VIC

How old is he?

JANELLE

Thirty-two. Why?

VIC

No, I mean the . . . your—

JANELLE

Dewey?

127

VIC

What kind of name's Dewey?

JANELLE

Almost twelve months.

VIC

I should never have came to L.A., Janelle.

JANELLE

Oh boy, here we go.

VIC

This isn't the kind of person you are. Cheating on people. Or me either. We're good people.

JANELLE

Here or in the living room?

VIC

I don't want no coffee. Where's my coat?

He gets to his feet and leaves the kitchen. JANELLE follows.

Living Room

VIC puts on his jacket, silhouetted in the half-light against the Hollywood nightscape, which glitters through the rain-washed windows.

VIC

Yeah wull, it's a pretty interesting place you got for yourself, Janelle, naked asses in the living room.

JANELLE comes forward to officiate at a Picasso drawing over the couch.

JANELLE

It's a Pablo Picasso.

VIC

Don't mean nothing to me.

JANELLE

Doesn't.

VIC

Shereen could do as good as that.

JANELLE

You don't mind my correcting you, do you?

VIC

Not if you don't mind I don't pay no attention.

JANELLE

It's not a weakness to talk good, Vic.

VIC

You can't even tell which is the woman and which is
the man.

JANELLE

Maybe they're neither, or maybe they're both.

VIC

Yeah, in Hollywood that's what they probably are,
is neither or both.

JANELLE

No, this is very interesting, Vic, this is very revealing. Why does it threaten you?

VIC

I'm glad you think so.

JANELLE

Why does your manhood have to depend on what
you can reject?

129

VIC

Just because I don't like naked asses in the living room, all of a sudden I'm revealing.

JANELLE

You won't let anything flower, will you?

VIC

Oh boy, Janelle, you sure got phony.

JANELLE

You won't let anything take hold and grow.

VIC

I'm just glad the people in Buddy can't hear you now.

JANELLE

That really bothers you, doesn't it?

VIC

Or see what's happened to you.

JANELLE

That I got out of Buddy and you're still stuck back there.

VIC

You make one record that nobody's ever heard of and, oh boy, she turns Hollywood.

JANELLE

That's right, go.

VIC

I'll see you, Janelle.

JANELLE

Into the night.

VIC

I got to find some place to stay, don't I?

JANELLE

There's just one thing I want to tell you, Vic, and then you can go.

VIC

Yeah?

JANELLE

Don't look so worried.

VIC

Hell, I ain't worried.

JANELLE

Do you want some coffee?

VIC

Aren't.

JANELLE

Let me turn off the coffee.

She returns to the kitchen.

VIC

Yeah, I'll have some coffee.

He goes after her.

Kitchen

JANELLE transfers the tray to the table and goes for the coffee as VIC sits down.

VIC

I should never have seen you again, Janelle, I know that much.

131

JANELLE

Don't be such a damn Boy Scout.

VIC

No, you're married. That's what you decided to do
and that's what you did.

JANELLE sits down and pours their coffee.

JANELLE

I was just as married fifteen minutes ago and I don't
remember it bothering you so much

VIC

It ain't my fault.

JANELLE

You're so sad.

VIC

Come on, Janelle, you're so phony.

JANELLE

You're the most pathetic person I've ever met.
(When he says nothing) Because you could be so
much and you won't be anything.

VIC

Oh yeah? When I get this bandage off, I'm going to
go to Pan America.

JANELLE

Vic, I love you, that's all. I never stopped. That's all
I have to say.

VIC

No, wull heck, I knew all we'd have to do is see each
other again and we'd be all over each other again all
over again.

JANELLE

That's not what I said, Bomber.

VIC

No, wull heck, I was going to say too that I didn't either, that I do too. Ever stop or anything.

He looks at her oddly, distantly, as though speaking of somebody else.

VIC

When you love someone you never stop or I don't know. Some things don't go away no matter where you go.

JANELLE

Are you going to stay?

VIC

I don't have no place else to go.

New Avenue Walkup Gym and Cultural Center

ARTY looks up from his desk, and if he is surprised to see VIC enter, his fixed look of dubious contempt conceals the fact.

VIC approaches, wagging his tail.

VIC

Hi, you old bastard, what do you say?

ARTY

What's your business? State your business.

VIC

Gee, what's the matter, Arty? I came in to see you. Thought I'd work out.

133

Five bucks a month to members.

He tosses an application at VIC.

Hell, Arty, come on.

This ain't no flophouse or free show.

Hell, if you weren't a friend of mine . . .

He reaches for a pencil.

What'll I put—Curley or Vic?

Whatever your name is, you put that down.

For the sake of peace, VIC makes a stab at the application.

Have to go pretty slow at first though, on account of
my hand got broke in this prison match up north,
knocking out this—

Five bucks, please.

Okay, Arty, when you get hungry I'll take care of
you. So don't go worrying about any five bucks for
crying out loud, what's five bucks?

He searches his pockets pointlessly for money.

I just didn't want to humiliate you with offering to

pay you, that's all. Here's fifty cents. I'm just going to watch today on account of my messed-up hand.

ARTY takes the fifty cents and slams it into his desk.

ARTY

Fucking bastards.

VIC

Boy, are you in a bad mood. If you weren't an old man I'd have to throw you downstairs.

ARTY assumes a fighter's stance.

ARTY

Come at me, motherfucker.

VIC

Hell, I wouldn't touch you. You'd probably have a heart attack and I can't afford flowers.

ARTY

What do you want?

VIC

Hell, man, I been finally thinking of going pro.

ARTY

Yeah, pro what?

VIC

So I might be looking for a good manager, so be careful.

ARTY

Happy hunting, asshole.

VIC

Just because I run out on you, Arty? Hell, I didn't run out on you. I had to go somewhere. I was coming back.

ARTY

I don't want you back.

VIC's face reddens.

VIC

You old fart. I wouldn't pay to take a crap in your fucking gym.

Tears flood his eyes and he turns and goes, almost running. ARTY pursues him across the room.

ARTY

Goddamn pain-in-the-ass free-loading zombie kids coming around hustling. I can spot them every time, Curley.

Los Angeles Streets

VIC storms from the gym and stalks the downtown streets flushed and tearful, too stunned to conceal his hurt.

Recording-Studio Hall

Do not enter when red light is flashing. This sign over a heavy soundproof door is flashing now on a still furious but less tearful VIC.

The light goes off and VIC pulls the door open and goes in.

Recording Studio

He ducks self-consciously before the glass horror of the engineer's booth and crosses to the corner, where large instruments are stored—cymbals, chimes and a piano.

DIRECTOR

(From the booth) Okay, sweetheart, wait a second. I'm coming out. It wasn't your fault.

In the still, shadowy room JANELLE in headphones is all alone at the mike. She stares at the floor in momentary fatigue and discouragement.

JANELLE

(Depressed) I can't get it.

She lights a cigarette and ducks wanly and little-girl-like into VIC's disinterested embrace as the DIRECTOR enters and proceeds to the mike to make adjustments.

JANELLE

(Babyish) I'm not any good.

VIC

I didn't even know you could sing.

He clears his throat, monumentally suppressed.

JANELLE

(Brightening) Did I tell you my new name? If at first you don't succeed in this business you change your name and start all over again. You okay?

VIC

What's your new name?

JANELLE

Candy Trick. What do you think of that?

VIC

You got to have a cute name, I guess.

JANELLE

Is something the matter?

VIC

That old fruit just wanted my ass, that's all.

DIRECTOR

(A warning mumble to JANELLE) The family's in the booth, luv.

JANELLE stiffens and steps away from VIC.

> VIC
>
> So I told him to shove it. He's not the only manager.

> JANELLE
>
> *(From the side of her mouth)* Don't look now, but Gary's in the booth.

> VIC
>
> Who's Gary?

And in spite of her warning, VIC looks.

> VIC
>
> Oh.

> JANELLE
>
> *(To the booth)* Honey? *(To the DIRECTOR)* Is this thing on?

> DIRECTOR
>
> Whenever you're ready, luv.

The DIRECTOR exits to the booth, ominous with engineers and echo effects and the shadowy presence of an injured party.

> JANELLE
>
> *(To the booth)* Honey, this is Vic Bealer from Buddy I was telling you about came down on a visit. *(To VIC)* Gary won't even believe there's a place called Buddy.

> DIRECTOR
>
> *(From the booth)* Any time, luv . . .

> JANELLE
>
> One last puff . . .

She inhales deeply and, with a caught moue only he can see, hands her cigarette to VIC.

> VIC
> (Through clenched jaw) Am I going to break his back or is he going to break mine?

> JANELLE
> Just don't clear your throat so much while I'm cutting, okay?

She returns to the mike, arranging her headset, as GARY DEARLY enters from the booth. One is at first startled that this is the man JANELLE has chosen, for he is next to VIC a peculiar second. Or is he? With the slight proud slink of certain dancers and beauticians, he clutches DEWEY to him as a weapon if not credentials, and one sees a small slight nature not unlike VIC's after all.

Demonstrating a threatening intention to be civilized, VIC joins GARY and stands beside him, rocking weirdly on the balls of his feet.

There's a false start in the prerecorded music and JANELLE eyes her husband and lover uneasily.

> VIC
> I didn't even know she could sing. I'm Vic.

> GARY
> (Indifferent if not serpentine) That remains to be seen.

> VIC
> I knew everything else about her but I didn't know that.

> JANELLE
> Okay, Bomber, don't go off the berserk. Just cool it. This is money here.

Everyone clears his throat of primitive impulses and the music starts.

JANELLE gets the beat and then leaps into her song. It's an overcute wail of teenage betrayal, and she's a verse or two into it when:

> VIC
> *(To* GARY*)* Did she tell you her new name?

> DIRECTOR
> *(From the booth)* Okay, hold it.

The music stops. JANELLE removes her headphones.

> JANELLE
> *(Seriously)* Vic . . .

She could be tougher but she sees now the devastation of his state of mind.

> VIC
> What?

> JANELLE
> You were talking.

> VIC
> I was talking?

> JANELLE
> Yes.

The DIRECTOR comes in and GARY goes out, taking DEWEY.

> VIC
> What was I saying?

> JANELLE
> Are you all right?

140

VIC

Wull, you know somebody always has something on
their minds.

JANELLE

Well, can it wait? *(To the* DIRECTOR*)* Okay.

The DIRECTOR departs.

VIC

No, I just said I think Candy Tooth is real great.
It's original.

JANELLE

Candy Trick.

VIC

Where did I get tooth?

JANELLE

Do you want to wait outside?

VIC

No, I'm fine. Yeah, sure, I'll be quiet. I just been hit
too many times. I'm punchy. I'll be quiet.

The music cues up and JANELLE takes her place. She looks
worriedly to the booth and shrugs.

VIC

I'll be quiet.

He looks around from side to side. He is sweating.

VIC

I'll be quiet.

Assuring all of good behavior, he walks backward into the
cymbals and chimes, overturning them loudly. An accident
or deliberate, it matters not. The result is the same: VIC is
the center of hostile attention and stricken with panic and
hurt.

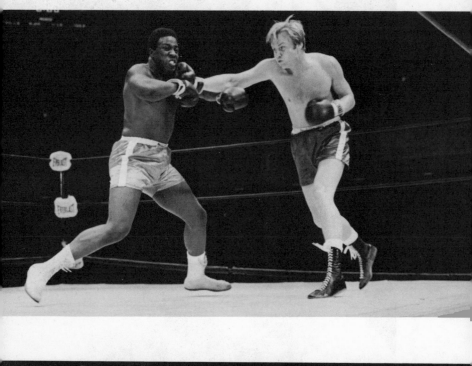

SIX

Buddy Boys' Club

Shadowboxing in worn silk shorts, VIC rubs sweat from his eyes and winces impatiently.

                    VIC
        Hey, Ariel, when you going to get something black
        to put up over the sun?

ARIEL crosses to do something about this annoyance.

HIGH VALENTINE, JOE SARAGUSA and a third Buddy booster, named KNIPCHILD, watch VIC at his workout, impressed and ingratiating. VALENTINE, DRENNA's father, is brittle and skinny in an Italian silk suit.

DRENNA, her hair in large rollers, sits by the ring on a folded mat and stares at VIC unhappily, a gray vigil, since he will not return her look.

ROCKOFF, it appears by his uniform, is now a policeman.

He lounges against the ropes at one end of the ring. Beyond him, through an open door, we see his police car and occasionally hear a shortwave summons that ROCKOFF ignores.

Present as well are two spindly Mexican kids smoking in a surly outcast manner that nonetheless expresses their awe of the great VIC BEALER. In the course of the scene these hangers-on become more at home and will begin to investigate the equipment and roll up their torn sleeves to reveal skinny arms straining for attention.

> ARIEL
>
> Hell, if you're not going to start training until six o'clock at night, I can't help it if the sun's so low it gets in your eyes.

He stands on an overturned crate and tries to cover the window with an old bathrobe.

> VIC
>
> (*With little breath*) Hell, man, you don't see me working out in here in the daytime. I'd burn myself up in here.

> DRENNA
>
> Do you know how hot it was today?

She is ignored.

> ARIEL
>
> Burn off that gut, you mean.

> VIC
>
> Look who's talking, man, with that spare tire.

> ARIEL
>
> Use that crouch, damn it. Don't just bend down. Come up with something.

VIC

(Grinning) Hell, I'm holding him off.

ARIEL

Holding him off—you're flat on your can.

VIC

You ever seen me on my can yet?

ARIEL

I'll put you there myself if you don't shut up and listen.

He winks at VALENTINE, SARAGUSA and KNIPCHILD, for whom, after all, this show is being presented.

DRENNA

(To no one in particular) One hundred and ten!

SARAGUSA

Trains great anyway.

ARIEL

Oh, don't let him fool you. The thing I got to watch out for is he don't go sour on me before the Nationals.

The sun still flashes in VIC's eyes.

VIC

Hell, man, hang something black up there or something.

ARIEL

Time.

VIC throws one final thrust at his nonexistent opponent.

VIC

(Breathing hard) How do you think I look, pretty damn good, huh?

ARIEL

You look lousy. (*To* VALENTINE, SARAGUSA *and*
KNIPCHILD) He looks lousy.

VIC

How many guys beat me so far? I can't remember.

ARIEL

Kids. They just give it to you.

VIC

Okay then, get me a fight with a fighter then.

ARIEL

(*To* VALENTINE, SARAGUSA *and* KNIPCHILD) See the
way he just pinpoints those shots?

VIC

Yeah, call me Sugar Ray.

He adjusts his radio to a scratchy rock 'n' roll.

ARIEL

You ain't no Sugar Ray.

VIC

If I had me a trainer . . .

DRENNA

I meant to ask you—do you want to see Ray Charles
on Friday?

VIC

Hey, come on, Rockoff, put on some trunks.

ROCKOFF

No, uh-huh, I'm on duty.

VIC

Come on. You can hit me and I won't put a glove
on you.

ARIEL

Time.

DRENNA

Just let me know so I can get tickets, okay?

VIC returns to the serious business of the workout.

HIGH

No, sir, you've done a real good job out here, Ariel,
no kidding. The Club looks really fine.

ARIEL

Well, it's just nothing but just secondhand junk I
just picked up.

HIGH

I had no idea, Knipchild, there was such a well-
equipped—

SARAGUSA

Nothing like it could be with a little push behind it,
High.

ARIEL

(To VIC) Downstairs, get him downstairs.

VIC

And drop my punch?

ARIEL

What punch?

VIC

Hell.

ARIEL

Get him in the heart. Throw one or two good ones
right to the heart and you got him paralyzed.

Looks pretty good, though, huh?

ARIEL

Oh Vic, oh sure, don't let him fool you.

KNIPCHILD

Looks good to me.

ARIEL

I'd just feel a lot easier in my mind, though, if he
was married is the only thing.

He drops a brief look to DRENNA.

SARAGUSA

More sense of responsibility.

ROCKOFF

(Laughing) Yeah, tied down.

SARAGUSA

More sense of his goals.

ARIEL

Because a white fighter without responsibilities is
not reliable. A middle-class white son-of-a-bitch
without goals will usually break your heart.

HIGH

You think he can win the Nationals at St. Louis?

They cluster closer to each other.

ARIEL

No, we're looking at a guy that's got what it takes.
That poor bastard right there could be on top.

Unable to hear clearly, ROCKOFF turns the radio down.

ROCKOFF

If he only wants to or what?

VIC

Don't touch my radio, man.

ROCKOFF

Hell, man, I got to hear my calls . . .

VIC climbs, threatening, out of the ring without waiting for ARIEL's "Time."

HIGH

(*To* ARIEL) What's the matter?

VIC

Don't nobody touch my radio but me.

ROCKOFF

Are you kidding?

ARIEL

Time.

VIC

If you want to hear another station or anything, just ask me, okay?

He turns the radio off and heads for the shower. The others exchange confounded, uneasy looks.

HIGH

Is something the matter?

ARIEL goes for his Pepto-Bismol.

ARIEL

The world's prima donna . . .

He gulps down a mouthful.

ARIEL

But there ain't no one I'd give you for him.

He recaps the bottle and notices for the first time one of the two Mexican kids.

ARIEL

What's your name, son?

The boy has put on gloves and stands by for approval.

ARIEL

(*To* HIGH) Any middleweight anyway, and half the heavyweights. You want to see him?

ARIEL leads HIGH to the dressing room, an eye cocked still to the newcomer who climbs into the ring and takes VIC's place.

HIGH

(*To* KNIPCHILD, *with reference to the* MEXICAN KID) When the goddamn N.A.C.P. gets through with everybody, if you want to go in and buy four white-wall tires I suppose it's going to be against the law if you don't get two black.

The MEXICAN KID puts his dukes up at the departing KNIP-CHILD.

KID

Hey, mon, want to fight?

KNIPCHILD trips over himself as he exits after HIGH and the others.

Dressing Room

VIC, in the shower, eyes the four men uneasily as they stand

158

across the room beyond the reach of splashing water appraising him, his total naked self.

SARAGUSA

If you'd seen him at San Francisco Civic, High, he really clobbered this . . . *(To* ARIEL) . . . what was it black or Mexican kid? Since he got out of the service, Arie, how many fights has he had? *(To* HIGH) And all but one was a knockout in the first or second.

KNIPCHILD

What happened then?

SARAGUSA

(Determined) This boy could put Buddy on the map, High, if he'd only just settle down.

HIGH steps toward the showers.

HIGH

What are your plans, Vic? Drenna's told us quite a lot about you, Mrs. Valentine and me, and we'd like to get to know you.

VIC steps slightly out of the shower, nervous but strangely resolute.

VIC

(Almost as though it was memorized) Wull . . . I won the Golden Gloves now twice, and what I thought was maybe I'd like to go to the Nationals this year in St. Louis, and then, I don't know, one day I guess the Olympics.

Approving the image, HIGH turns to the others and nods.

HIGH

The good old U.S.A.

The greatest thing of all, I have always thought, would be to just be standing there for the United States and see the American flag go up when they play *The Star-Spangled Banner*.

He steps back under the water, and spray flies out over HIGH.

VIC

And after that, hell, why not? The world can have me.

Kezar Stadium, San Francisco

The fights have already begun, and threading their way through the thick crowd pushing to get inside, we recognize first HIGH and MAGDA VALENTINE, and following them VIC and DRENNA. HIGH and MAGDA are very drunk and therefore stiff and cautious.

HIGH

What time . . . are we late?

As though looking for the host, he holds his tickets aloft, the ignored passport of his doubtful right to be. His hand is trembling.

VIC

Just the preliminaries . . .

MAGDA

Hey, they got beer.

DRENNA

Mother.

MAGDA

Hey! Beer!

DRENNA

Mother . . .

MAGDA

Over here!

DRENNA

Motherrrrrrr!

MAGDA

(Through her teeth) What is it?

DRENNA quickens her pace to pick up her mother's drooping, almost dragging mink. She replaces it on MAGDA's shoulders in a gesture that is all but strangling.

VIC takes up the rear of this group, spruced and empty-eyed and smelling of Command; he wears a tapered shirt and booty shoes and, alas, we see in a crowd he is one of many similar young men.

Ringside

Smoky and serious, the atmosphere is typical of the early hours of a championship event. The crowd is full of nervous blood lust. People visit excitedly and collect empty beer cups under their seats.

Coming down the aisle:

MAGDA

Where's the guy from Fresno? I'm for him.

DRENNA

Sacramento.

I'm for him.

She would continue on to the ring itself, but HIGH grabs her.

These are just the preliminaries, Mag.

They move sideways into seats eight rows back.

I thought you said ringside. We could have paid ten dollars and had better seats than this.

Hey, there's Dixie Gang . . .

Supporting himself for a moment on a stranger's shoulder, HIGH gestures toward the ring.

Dixie . . . over here.

As they crowd into their seats, MAGDA pushes DRENNA aside in order to have VIC for herself.

Dixie Gang's taking on your father. Don't forget to congratulate him. He was with Nixon all through California. And you'll get a bang out of this, Vic. You know who else's his client?

She pulls on HIGH, who is stretching to meet DIXIE GANG.

What's his name, honey, who Mr. Gang represents, the fighter?

Joe DiMaggio.

162

MAGDA

(To VIC*)* Joe DiMaggio.

DIXIE GANG is a bald boy of forty, with a non-stop smile.

HIGH

. . . my son-in-law, *future* son-in-law, and that little
lady is my daughter. And you know Mag.

MAGDA

We were supposed to be up at ringside.

HIGH

This is ringside. All this is ringside.

DIXIE scans the crowd for better connections.

DIXIE

(Calling) Hey, Bobo . . . Bobo Olson. Over here.

VIC

(To DRENNA, *gulping)* There's Bobo Olson.

HIGH

You want to take a good look at Vic here, Dixie.
He's the kid I was telling you was going to St. Louis
in a couple of weeks.

DIXIE

(Wants to get away) How about having lunch next
week, High? *(To* MAGDA*)* We're going to put this old
man of yours in Sacramento or bust.

MAGDA

He won't learn. Three times he's run and three
times he's lost.

HIGH

You got to be a crook to win. I'm just not crook
enough, that's all.

163

MAGDA

Politics! Count me out.

DIXIE looks for a point of departure.

HIGH

You're the crook.

MAGDA

I'm the one that ought to run. I'd win for a change.

HIGH

Long as it's not a beauty contest.

MAGDA

First thing he's got to learn how to do is get people decent seats. We were supposed to be ringside.

DIXIE

It's been a pleasure meeting all you nice people.

He escapes and HIGH shakes MAGDA's fur at her, squeezing it to death.

HIGH

He got me these seats. Dixie Gang got me these seats and wouldn't take a dime, Mag, for crying out loud.

MAGDA

Hey, beer! Here.

The VENDOR stops.

MAGDA

Am I the only one? Are you guys just going to sit and watch me?

VENDOR

You're the one I'm looking for, lady.

MAGDA

I'm out with a bunch of pansies. Pay the man, honey.

She leans forward.

MAGDA

Come on, White Trunks.

She leans against VIC.

MAGDA

I got White Trunks. What color trunks are you on, Vic?

HIGH

Come on, Green Trunks.

MAGDA

He's just leaning on White Trunks. (*To the ring*) Hey you, stand on your own two feet, why don't you? (*To* HIGH) He's not even bleeding.

VIC

(*Almost to himself*) He's just waiting to throw one to the jaw and meanwhile he's getting beat.

HIGH

Atta boy, Green Trunks, kill him.

MAGDA

What do you mean, atta boy? He's getting the worst of it.

HIGH

Yeah yeah, your boy.

MAGDA

Your boy, you mean.

DRENNA puts her hand in VIC's.

VIC

They're just tired. That's what the trouble is.

HIGH

What are they, just amateurs? This is a professional fight.

MAGDA

Come on, White Trunks, let's retaliate.

HIGH

He's finished. *(Up)* Knock his ass out of there. That's it, push him over, nail him.

The bell rings.

White Trunks is slumped in his corner, his silks water-soaked and pink with blood. He's exhausted. His trainer crouches before him, doctoring cuts on his face. VIC watches.

MAGDA

Where's that beer man? Don't you boys want a little drinkie?

Her hand clutches VIC's knee. DRENNA, on his other side, leans against him and clings, as though this pressure would relieve his discomfort.

HIGH

Raring to go there, Bomber? Getting any pointers?

Now MAGDA's claw moves up VIC's leg and under a dangled end of mink she gropes his privates thoughtfully.

MAGDA

When are we going to see you in action, son-of-a-bitch? Getting excited?

VIC turns, stricken, to DRENNA. But she pleads ignorance of this outrage and simply smiles, albeit pretty weakly.

SEVEN

Bealer House

A small and shabby living room, with toys and dolls the décor.

We see into the dining room, where RODINE is cleaning a child from the effects of a meal. SHEREEN comes in from this direction and sits down next to VIC on the couch.

He is recently out of the shower and wears only slacks and a towel around his neck.

NOLA enters from the kitchen. She is dressed up and we observe that there is a company note to SHEREEN and RODINE as well. NOLA carries VIC's shoes, newly shined.

> NOLA
> *(Calling his bluff)* If you're really not going I wish you'd of let me know before I shined these.

> VIC
> I'm not going.

Well, I am. Just to see the tears in everyone's eyes when you don't show up.

I don't even know what I'm going for.

He starts to put on his shoes.

You just got to learn to think more high of yourself, don't he, Rodine?

RODINE comes into the living room carrying a slow two-year-old.

You earned all this, Vic. This is what you wanted and this is what you got. And you're entitled to take it. Now hurry up.

God will take you by the hand.

Once pretty, RODINE is now tightly combed and limply sweatered in permanent touch-me-not mourning that submits only to the tyranny of her young.

The only reason I'm going, though, is so that they all don't come out here.

I'm not ashamed of where I live and you shouldn't be either.

I wouldn't have a maid if I could afford one.

Look where we live. It's just a dump.

Well, you can change all that. It's in your hands.

(Accusingly) Yeah, marry a rich girl.

NOLA

(Stung) Drenna's a nice girl. I don't care who she is.

RODINE

Where'd they come up with a name like Drenna?

SHEREEN

Is Uncle Vic going to get married?

VIC

You can shut up, Shereen, or you don't get to go.

NOLA hands him his shirt.

NOLA

You're not going to stop people loving you, Vic, so you just better get used to the idea.

She tries to help him on with it.

NOLA

Because I don't know no one don't like you and don't think the best of you unless it's Vic Bealer himself.

SHEREEN

I don't.

A car honks outside.

VIC

(Electrified) Who is it?

RODINE looks out.

RODINE

Looks like everybody.

VIC

Goddamn it.

NOLA

What's the matter?

VIC

I scratched a hickey. Am I bleeding?

NOLA

You're not bleeding.

VIC

Under my titty.

She inspects it.

VIC

(Panicked) Heck no, I'm bleeding.

NOLA

It's all right.

RODINE comes in to examine the wound, followed by
SHEREEN.

VIC

Aw, shit.

NOLA

Vic—

VIC

I got something in my eye.

NOLA

Let's see.

VIC

Where's my radio?

They surround him, NOLA at his eye, RODINE and SHEREEN
investigating his right chest.

VIC

Would it be possible to just be let alone if you don't
mind?

170

Swooze Car Interior

JAY DAVID drives, with CONNIE and ARIEL in the front seat. VIC is in back, flanked by BETT and DRENNA. They head through Buddy, a caravan of a dozen or so cars sometimes in view behind them.

CONNIE

When's the big day? Have you decided?

DRENNA

When he gets home we'll decide.

VIC

She may not want me any more after I come back all messed up.

DRENNA

He better not.

BETT

Well, hurry up so Ariel can rely on you.

ARIEL

I can rely on him.

VIC

He can rely on me.

BETT

Show Connie the ring Dren gave you.

ARIEL

Don't bug him, Bett. Lay off if all you have to ask him is questions. I don't want him all bugged.

VIC

How long does a helicopter take from Buddy to San Francisco anyway?

171

BETT

Doesn't anybody want to see this ring?

vic holds his hand toward the front seat, ring finger elevated.

VIC

It's a rattlesnake.

CONNIE

Beautiful. Is that pure gold?

VIC

They had a matching pair and she thought I was
going to buy her one, that's how dumb she is.

DRENNA

Je vous aime, mon amour. Je vous adore.

There is a startled dull silence. Then:

JAY DAVID

Hell, he'll win tomorrow night, no doubt about
that. But you'll be sure to call us right up after,
Bomber, won't you? Reverse.

CONNIE

And then goodbye freedom. What does Mother say?

VIC

Wull heck, no, hell . . . it's bound to be better
than just cutting out all the time and going around
and living off the lay of the land all the time like I
been. I'm looking forward to it, settling down, I
really am.

He clears his throat so completely it all but detaches his
uvula.

Buddy County Airport

This is nothing more than a grassy field used sometimes by private planes. Right now, as the caravan pulls into it, there is a helicopter waiting some distance away.

JAY DAVID, CONNIE, ARIEL, BETT, DRENNA and VIC get out of the Swooze car and head for the helicopter, VIC with his plaid plastic suitcase. NOLA, RODINE and SHEREEN arrive in another car.

SHEREEN catches up with VIC and DRENNA, who is reading from a notebook page tugged from her tomboy pocket.

> DRENNA
>
> Riches are ephemeral
> And beauty but a phase.
> I would gladly give up everything
> To live three precious days.
>
> Just three days I can love you in,
> I ask no more than that,
> And that shall be enough for me
> Even though you don't love me back.

> VIC
>
> Come on, Drenna, I said I did.

> DRENNA
>
> I would live but three days gladly,
> Then face my life of sorrow,
> For I would love you madly—

> SHEREEN
>
> (*Jumping in with the obvious punchline*) Yesterday, today and tomorrow.

HIGH comes forward from the helicopter to greet them, followed by MAGDA, SARAGUSA, KNIPCHILD and other important Buddians. ROCKOFF, in uniform, is here to prevent riot.

HIGH puts his arm around VIC for posterity as PARKER snaps the picture.

>HIGH
>
>We're counting on you, Vic, to win now, so don't disappoint us.

>VIC
>
>I just wish you'd asked me to do my best, Mr. Valentine.

MAGDA separates DRENNA from VIC and moves in beside him as they continue toward the helicopter.

>MAGDA
>
>He's like me. He's got a strong arm and a good punch and nobody's beat us yet, have they, Victor?

BETT gives ARIEL a big wet kiss and ARIEL, looking at the helicopter, rubs his stomach.

>ARIEL
>
>If I could just throw up.

Behind ARIEL is the MEXICAN KID from the Boys' Club, combed and spiffy, followed by his family.

And coming next are CONNIE and JAY DAVID huffing and puffing in the heat.

Signs read: Good Luck, Vic. Buddy's Own Vic Bealer. Vote For Valentine. And less impressive signs in Spanish try to do as much for the MEXICAN KID.

The High School Drill Team, set in motion at the outset and now forgotten, marches out across the open field past the helicopter, whose turning blades flatten the grass and make everyone shout.

NOLA kisses VIC.

NOLA

(Shouting) There's a fine golden sun bursting over your head, Vic, and little Drenna, and it's not just a mother talking.

CONNIE

(Shouting) Did you see his ring?

ARIEL moves VIC toward the helicopter.

ARIEL

(Sickly) We don't want to miss the plane, Bomber.

BETT

Hey, I haven't kissed Marlon goodbye yet.

She gives VIC a gooey kiss and then twists him around to DRENNA.

BETT

There, I warmed him up for you.

DRENNA stares into VIC's face.

DRENNA

Je t'aime, Veek.

VIC

I will.

DRENNA

Et Dieu est avec vous.

VIC kisses NOLA. He hugs CONNIE. RODINE, clutching artificial daisies, moves in for her farewell. VIC ignores her and turns to JAY DAVID, who steps backward and extends a paw.

> JAY DAVID
>
> Just a formal handshake will be just fine for me,
> thanks.

ROCKOFF throws their suitcases into the helicopter. ARIEL
helps the MEXICAN KID in and then turns to VIC as PARKER
lies on the ground to get an arty shot of ROCKOFF pumping
VIC's hand.

> ROCKOFF
>
> Give em hell, Bomber, okay?

> VIC
>
> Whatever you say, Andy.

> ROCKOFF
>
> *(Moved to tears)* No hell, I mean it. Me and Lov-
> ette give five dollars for toward the fund so you
> could go . . . *(Thinks this is encouraging)* . . . so
> I mean we got a stake in you, buddy, so don't let us
> down, okay?

VIC looks at him and smiles weirdly, in that sinister satisfaction that comes to him now and then when he can take no
more and suddenly finds the way out. ARIEL reaches down
and helps him into the helicopter.

The crowd retreats as the helicopter prepares to take off. It
rises. RODINE rushes forward and flings her daisies into a
maelstrom of dust and weed. People clutch their clothes
and grin into the sky. The helicopter gains altitude and
leans toward the mountains in the west. This is indeed a
great day for Buddy. One of their own is headed for fame.

Helicopter's Point of View

As it rises above the crowd, it brings into view the straggling Drill Team spread over the field and all the world looking up at VIC, RODINE at the center, fanatic and faithful.

Helicopter Interior

Breathing deeply to control his nausea, ARIEL tries to smile.

> ARIEL
>
> Well, we're finally off, I guess, huh? Goodbye to Buddy, hello the world.

He looks to VIC, scowling at his side.

> VIC
>
> Let's go down.

The PILOT reacts vaguely.

> ARIEL
>
> What?

> VIC
>
> Put the thing down.

> ARIEL
>
> We got to catch a plane out of Frisco at four o'clock, Bomber. What did you forget?

> VIC
>
> I ain't going.

The plane continues on course and the PILOT looks at the silent ARIEL.

> PILOT
>
> What do I do?

> VIC
>
> You put the damn thing back down on the ground like I told you to.

177

ARIEL

(Sighing) Take her down.

Buddy County Airport

A look of longing and happy grief still lingers on the faces below.

But now expressions begin to change to confusion and then to alarm as people observe the helicopter descend again some distance out in the fields.

Some begin to move quickly in that direction; CONNIE, JAY DAVID, BETT and ROCKOFF hobble over the rough terrain. HIGH, MAGDA, SARAGUSA, KNIPCHILD look dumbly at each other and then turn to VALENTINE's car. It zooms off, however, without them, DRENNA at the wheel.

Left behind is NOLA. Strangely, she does not look surprised or shocked. If anything, there is a look of good-humored sadness on her face. RODINE joins her, her satisfaction unconcealed. They stare at the distant helicopter and the many running for it, the Drill Team having a considerable lead.

At the Helicopter

VIC has got down from the plane and stands with his suitcase in his hand as ARIEL circles him screaming.

ARIEL

You bring them along, you take them along and give them the best you got and then just when there's a chance to make something out of it all, they cop out on you and you got nothing.

VIC

It's just wrong, Ariel. It's just all wrong.

ARIEL

Yeah, that's amateur for you—always stay where you can run.

VIC

Yeah wull, that's professional for you too—someone telling you what to do the rest of your life.

ARIEL

Vic, someone's going to be telling you what to do one way or another.

He goes behind a tree to throw up or otherwise relieve himself. VIC looks to the distant Buddians hurrying toward him across the field.

VIC

I don't want to talk to them all, Arie.

ARIEL returns, still critically queasy.

ARIEL

That's just a illusion you kids got, that you're free.

VIC

No one's going to own me, that's all.

ARIEL

You're not free. No more'n the rest of us. You're about as free as I don't know what, because you're bugged, Vic.

VIC

I ain't bugged.

ARIEL

You're standing back. Afraid to take a chance that is offered to you to go all the way. Sure, it's going to cost you something, but if you think you're free just because you're drifting around and no one's got a

179

hold on you, that's not free, Bealer, that's caught.

VIC

(*Smiles*) Take it easy, Ariel. You're talking so fast you'll have a heart attack.

ARIEL takes a breath and holds his heart and then lets go again.

ARIEL

I think you're chicken.

VIC

You can think that.

ARIEL

That's what I think.

VIC

There ain't no one I can't beat and you know it. And I give them ten or twenty pounds. And I know that so damn well that I don't ever have to get up and try and prove it.

ARIEL looks back at the approaching crowd and time is all but gone. The PILOT reacts anxiously, wanting to know what to do.

ARIEL

This may rock you a bit, Vic, but I'm no seventeen-year-old girl that'll believe anything and what you just said don't mean a damn thing. Even to yourself. You're just a punk who don't have nothing to put back into the game and you're just scared now people are on to you.

VIC says nothing.

ARIEL

And well, I'm not missing my chance.

He starts back to the helicopter.

180

And I'm not wasting no more time on punks who'll only fight so they don't have to work steady at nothing and live off their loyalties or royalties or laurels or whatever you want to call them of a few amateur fights in a Boys' Club or rehabilitation prison meets—

VIC

Arie . . .

ARIEL stops and VIC comes to him. He holds out his hand to say goodbye. ARIEL doesn't take it.

ARIEL

I'm sorry, Vic. That's the way I feel about it. So all their lives they could tell themselves they could have been something. And who'll ever know the difference.

He climbs up into the helicopter.

ARIEL

Let's go.

Open Fields

People stop in their tracks as the helicopter suddenly takes to the air again. Some want to believe all is well now. Others cannot.

Only DRENNA keeps on going, bumping along over the rough ground in the family car. When the car flounders, she gets out and runs.

Distant Fields

VIC marches along with his trusty suitcase. DRENNA tries to keep pace with him but it is difficult.

DRENNA

(Breathless) True love is waiting and hoping and praying and sacrificing, Vic, and being happy and not being afraid.

VIC

Who says I'm afraid?

DRENNA

Keep smiling, Vic, because our love is strong enough to face any problem that faces us, I know that—

VIC

I don't love you.

She falters.

VIC

I just seen you coming, that's all.

He continues on.

DRENNA's strength renews and she hurries after him.

DRENNA

Because the search for happiness is one of the hardest things in life to find. But when you find it with a person . . . I may be young, Vic, but I know what I'm talking about.

VIC

You're just asking for it, Drenna. Go away!

DRENNA

Because true love is good times *and* bad, Vic. It's consideration and sharing and understanding and praying together and waiting, Vic, and sitting down and talking and doing what the other one wants—

VIC

Go on, Drenna, go home.

Are you just going to leave me hanging in mid-air, not knowing if it's over or what?

He stops, in order to make it quite clear.

VIC

It's over. Goodbye.

Then he proceeds.

DRENNA follows.

DRENNA

It's this not knowing, Vic.

But she hasn't the strength to keep up.

DRENNA

I feel like you're pushing me away and I'm just supposed to hang here in mid-air . . .

She can't go on. Crying, she watches him grow smaller against the dry fleshy field.

DRENNA

And the dumb part is I really do understand and don't really expect you to jump on any white horse and carry me off . . .

VIC is by this time far into the landscape, leaving her behind and in the distance the rest of Buddy.

The Road from Buddy

This is the two-lane country road we have seen in the beginning, not widely used. It stretches in both directions through eventless countryside.

There is a small bridge that spans a dry wash here, and

seated on the concrete wall is VIC. There is nothing in sight in any direction except fields and a few low hills. He is entirely alone. His expression is blank and if anything a little incredulous, chagrined.

Though he is isolated and far from home and without shelter, and though in a moment it might rain, and though he is hurt and he hasn't eaten, he has not yet thought to be worried or concerned. Some say VIC is not bright enough to come in out of the rain. Others admire and envy that character that is stronger than the changes in weather or the pangs of hunger, whose confidence is rooted in a physical strength and the capacity to endure.

He looks around at the barren realm of his homeland and the silence is the silence of nature alone, accented by the scratching of a bird or rodent somewhere out of sight among the rocks, the rasping of the wind through dry weed. It is ominous. And then there is the sound of a car coming.

VIC stands up and puts his suitcase at his feet. He waits and smiles faintly at the oncoming car.

What is he smiling at? Why did he smile so often, so unusually during our acquaintance? Is there something funny? It has always seemed a little taunting, a little threatening, a little mean. We guess it is VIC's wont to smile. Or that he smiles out of shyness or embarrassment or when he thinks an uncomplimentary thought. Or because he was taught to smile. Or because of all things the smile is the most disarming and the most protective of expressions.